scavenger

scavenger

a novel by
dennison smith

INSOMNIAC PRESS

Edited by Mike O'Connor
Copy edited by Lloyd Davis & Liz Thorpe
Designed by Mike O'Connor

Canadian Cataloguing in Publication Data

Smith, Dennison
      Scavenger

ISBN 1-895837-15-4

PS3569.M524S64 1997   813'.54   C97-931372-4

The publisher gratefully acknowledges the support of the
Ontario Arts Council.

Printed and bound in Canada

Insomniac Press
378 Delaware Ave.
Toronto, Ontario, Canada, M6H 2T8

with gratitude and love to Jenny Parker, Henry Parker Jr.
and Grandma Shorty of the Navajo Nation, Arizona.

further acknowledgements

Thanks to Ella Mike, Sandy Mike, and Yazze BigMan of the Navajo Nation for all they taught me. Thanks to Homer Parker for translating for Jenny. To Kate and Mark Sorenson and Greg Shepherd for help, introduction, patience and shelter. To Mary Baldwin Stoner and Susan Stoner of Phoenix for books and comfort. Grateful acknowledgement to the years of field research of the ethnographers: Gladys Reichard, Father Berard Haile, John Farella, Gary Witherspoon, Charotte Frisbie. And especially to Matthew Remski, for the unchartable.

introduction

Scavenger was born to become a god, but, like so many saviours, at first was a slave. He survived on scraps from the table and the dung pile and the dog's lair and the stables, and so was called Scavenger, The-One-Who-Goes-About-Picking-Up-Discarded-Things. Sometimes he was called The-One-Who-Is-Rough because he was worked till he scarred. His masters sent him into terrible places. In a bucket strung by yucca rope and hooked over a juniper branch, they raised him up to the Cliffs of the Dead, there to steal the eagle's eggs and die at the eagle's talons.

But the wind loved him. Though this action of wind is unrecorded, yet the wind loved him as I love him, because he was beautiful. The wind said, Beg the eagle's mercy. And he did. The eagle mother pitied Scavenger. She wrapped him in her giant wings. He became as one of her own. She brought him water in bowls tied to her tail and talons. She brought him the flesh of mountain sheep, gored with her claws. She brought her beak to the wound and then to his mouth. She offered her mouth and Scavenger ate. Feeding on dead things delivered with love, Scavenger grew up deadly and beautiful.

He was raised in an eagle's nest, and brought to the sky as one born there. Time came for the eagles to rise through the hole in the world and live in the sky which is the crown of these worlds. There are many worlds, as you will see, each with its exit. The wind with all that it carries, and the gods that come and go like small stories, and everything that ever flies, all these move easily between the worlds. Because Scavenger did not move easily, the eagles prepared to carry him up. They painted his face with white clay and wrapped his body in blue cloud. They bound him with lightning bolts and rainbows strung around a hammock of clouds. They gave him a crystal for light and a reed for breath. They raised him up. But he was heavy. And when the eagles tired, their wings drenched with raindrops, they asked for help of the snakes. They lent the snakes several feathers so the snakes wouldn't fall down to earth. This way the snakes flew. This way the eagles and the snakes together carried Scavenger through the sky hole. This way, Scavenger became holy, by that which flies and that which slithers, despite his birth.

blood, bonnets, and
lightning-that-extends-away

My mother was born in an abattoir. I believe it was an ugly scene. Slabs of cow hung like candelabra throwing black light; biting flies, a blue-green adornment on meat, sawdust floor of gut, leather boot, and the ladies wore white aprons. They bent over my grandmother's body like a dream of stars. She had fled hunger in Ireland, grown pregnant in New York. It was 1863. I have skipped at least one generation, but, in this history, which is mine, only the minutes between contractions are important.

In a chamber of torsos sliced lengthwise, amongst drippings and mutterings in obscure tongues, two women lifted my grandmother's weight, and plied her palms around an empty meat hook. A blood-drenched hand plunged scummed fingers into my grandmother's vulva and grabbed hold of the tight-sheathed head. My grandmother gave birth. Head, fist, neck, elbow, the baby came out punching, mealy and soaked in incubus sack. Shoulder, other elbow, blood, other fist, hot wet heart, lungs, blister over the nipple, stomach, limp umbilical that would fall away like a raisin in the cradle cord, rump, miniscule vagina, anus, urethra, fat white thighs streaming, knees, sickle calves, bath-toes, toenails. The women dragged it out. It was my mother. It had red hair.

What was her father's name? He could have been the devil. Or an angel, and my mother could not bear the brightness of his eyes and the holiness of his song and so she went mad, being frail. He could have been the wind itself, who struggles in her throat tonight. Soon you will hear her screaming from the family room. One day, I will try to understand these things.

But today I am six. I am swinging on a swingset. I am hanging from my family tree in the garden. Bird's nest in the cholla. I jump off. I play. I put a yellow paper beak over my hand, drop my paints in the dirt, and feed myself. I am Scavenger. It is time to ascend. I am the condor who taught all humans to fly, but humans have forgotten how to subdue the air.

When I find dead birds in the desert, I cut their wings off with my pocket knife. I have many colours of wings. They will suffice to describe me. And in my bedroom, I have a dictionary, and a window over this garden I name **gethsemane** (from olive press): a place or occasion of great mental or spiritual suffering.

Subdued, I stand so still that the air cannot hear the wind in me. Then slowly, so slowly, I move my fingers with no rings, my palm with no lines, my wrists, no bracelet, motion through to my elbows and the soft behind my elbows, tremor of my biceps, my shoulders, and I begin to fly.

Age seven, I remake the moment by my own flashing light. Some say I am the child of the Devil. No seven-year-old thinks like this. It is nineteen-seventy, the suburbs, Phoenix, Arizona, America, land of amnesia, and I am a wide generation away from all true stories.

history

Let me recount my lineage. I will count backwards from the Virgin Mary. Mary was the daughter of Anne, born without sin. The book tells me nothing else but to revere her and stop asking. But let me indulge in ancestor worship. Anne was the daughter of Peggy who dressed blithely as whomever she pleased. Let me unclothe her. She swapped clothes with a soldier to enliven a party. She would have swapped clothes with a rabbi if she could find one willing to swap. She kept time and beat and inverted whatever went solid. She was the pendulum. She made a room aware of itself. She made a room slip through doors, do limbo naked under the stars. The ugly stop longing for mirrors. She was the mirror. It warbled. And the deaf heard water with dripping lobes. The ceiling swung. She was the bell. Someone kissed her pinkie, she never caught his name. She was a prayer some said, but no one heard the words. Sometimes she muttered. Some said she was a witch. She had a bottomless cup given to her by a foreigner whose scent was bitter. She was thirsty, and she was never hungry. She hated the strings of meat. She hated the flatness of sugar. She could never sleep, and she never dreamt, though she imagined there was no waking up from this dream, for she was to dream the world from the womb of her daughter.

Peggy was a butcher's wife which is not such an ugly thing in a necessary world. Peggy and her husband were happy with child and put handprints of lamb's blood on her corrugated belly. This was the mark of the future, every finger a limb of the apple tree of the past pointing upward toward the fallen Eve who had begun this solemn lineage downward. Let me model myself on Peggy.

Peggy was the daughter of Lucinda, and Lucinda cooked aubergines, standing straight in the spray of the grease, she mortified herself and fed her family. Lucinda's mother Gertrude lived with her daughter and son-in-law and made a nuisance of domestic advice that fortified all living creatures in the radius of explosion. Gertrude was born with no complications from the womb of Charlotte, who was a churning stew of stinking fish. Being that hot and rotten, Charlotte returned at the age of eighty into the Mediterranean after years of concentrated mutation. Charlotte was the daughter of Mohab and Serabel, exemplary peasantry who never rioted and spawned males furiously. Charlotte was their one daughter to survive ritual strangulation. Serabel was reared of Susie who grew lemons and was said to have been impregnated by a wasp. Susie was born to Alexandria who was a state. Alexandria descended after forty-two continuous hours of pushing, while gripping an olive stump, from her mother's exceptionally small vagina. Great cries were said to be heard across the empire. The mother's name was Doris. Doris had blonde hair like Doris Day and had come out of the woods followed by a herd of deer, all of whom she called by tender names. After this, she moved to town and lost her innocence. Doris' mother Gochef never married but was raped. Gochef was born of Matilda who was the origin of the dance and refused to pumice her feet. Matilda was the child of Esther who was a single mother and confined to a reed cell while her daughter was given over to soldiers with helmets on their cocks. Esther was the daughter of a mother named Puba whose name was laughable until she martyred herself for the sake of an insect. Puba was born in a cave in which her mother, Isador, sucked stalactites because of overwhelming thirst during drought. The rest of her mother's village died. Puba and Isador survived eating grubs, and she would always feel she owed her life to grubs. Isador was the offspring of Saman the nomad who moved her long skirt like a sidewinder across the desert, leaving tracks beyond death. Saman sprung from the mouth of her mother, Liba, who was a great river and died only when she reached the sea. Liba's mother was Notek who was mud. Notek's mother was a queen whose name was taken away from her because she misused it. The Queen's mother was Gold, and Gold was so beautiful she raised two armies of four thousand and sang to them from her elevation among the foxtail cliffs, as the armies ran into each other's axes and died. In the night she would make love to the most beautiful corpse, and the most beautiful corpse would become an eternal statue in Gold's country. Gold's mother was very pure, hallmarked by huge grey eyes that looked with sadness as the ravens came to feast upon the younger generation, and she said, because of this atrocity I will make the night scream to cover all human weeping. Her name was O. O was the daughter of Dawn who could never be called a coward. Dawn was freckled and full of grace and, though she emerged in the nether regions, hearing the groaning of the substance that bore her, she did not blame the beginning for the bad rations. Dawn ran from one side of the world to the other, looking for her mother, The Night. The Night was called The Night because she was the only one of the jet-black women to open her mouth into a perfect circle and reveal her white teeth. When she smiled the moon waxed. She was the daughter of the hour before Eve. Who was said to have had no mother.

(my own mother was beautiful before she went mad)

mother and liquid

I am in the garden and a red bird flies beyond my small hand,
lands on the cholla, and the cholla blossoms. I see my mother
through the sliding glass door at her desk. She is writing with
red ink. Mother is beautiful. It is spring and the first monsoon.
The sky is open with rain. The season floods, unable to absorb
its whim. The worms rise and are thoroughly beaten, and the
birds come down to feed and bruise themselves on raindrops.
What are you doing inside, mommy? I am drenched in the yard, in my
yellow rain boots. A cat springs out of the cat-hole. Where do creatures come from, mommy? It is scuffling its tight moist features over
my loose rubber ankle. It purrs. Its spine moons, or like a fish
tail, curls in an endless swim. Its body around my boot-feet, like
a current conformed to the scattering of rocks. I am caressed at
eight years old. There is a feeling of sex on my toes and a pulsing
in my bladder. The cat's empty throat is full of hunger, small
vocal cords trilling. Then, humping, claws in the rubber, pump
pump. I shake the cat off as if it were a bird, and run in through
the sliding glass doors. I knock over the red ink my mother is
using for correction. My mother was a kindergarten teacher. She
liked a fine nib fountain pen. She liked to draw the happy faces
in the corner of the colouring project: Noah's ark, cows, horses,
deer, bears, apes, man, no woman, no cat, no lizard, no condor,
no eagles, no snakes, no ants, no tarantula hawk, no scorpions,
nothing real-life. I didn't think it was a very good picture. But
suddenly it was gone as if the sea rose up above it and drowned
it, dead giraffes, bloated carcass, red ink everywhere. It was the
monsoon season.

I say to mother, There was a cat and I need to pee. I pee. I
should at this moment begin to menstruate if fiction were perfect, but I am
much too young. The sunset ochres with black rain, my mother
soaks in red ink, I have pissed on the floor. Everything seeming
to work in a great coalition; cat, avatar, catalyst, monsoon and
Noah. Painting, piss, and the deep plush carpet. Red ink, moth-

er's burnt hands; furrows of red, shooting veins, heading for the heart, and possible blood clot. Boom. Was that thunder? But my mother, for a moment, looked beautiful because she was exposed by colour.

(when I begin to menstruate it will be like this:)

I squat in my window, with my labia clanging, blood dripping down mortar, descending vertical like Virginia Creeper failing in the climate. My blood will be acid. Vermilion. Blood down the vine, wrapping itself like Saturn around the house. My blood cuts. Cleans. It is phosphorus. Phosphine. Forms salt. It is Basic Orange 15. It has tendrils. It coagulates and rolls. It is mercury, cinnabar, brilliant red crystal, roasted calomel. It is acid alizarin. Pigment Red 60. It is reddening litmus. It is boric. Sulphuric. It is brimstone. The stone walls of the yellow house corrode. Acetic acid made by fermentation of alcohol and the distillation of wood. It is acetic anhydride, a colourless mobile liquid with a pungent odour and lachrymatory action. It is ferment. It is colourless only when pure. Tricholoroacetic, it is virtually complete. Nitric, it is colourless, and continues to pour through the glass, down the gutter head, evolving into hydrogen, spewing out the mouth, hydrated to hydronium ion, and into the rushing sewers to wash away everything.

Red ink ran across my mother's wrists as piss dripped down my thighs. I didn't know what to say to her. The little reindeer tried to kill the dragon with a gun, I said. This is a cloud, this is the dragon, and it's all red. I pointed to a stained picture, smiling. Then I pointed to a blank sheet on the other side of the desk, untouched by the ink spill. Look, mommy, it's the desert and it's white.

My mother looks out the sliding glass door, through the aluminium frame. No trees to spoil the desert view, no autumn leaves in the wind like ghosts cursing or sighing for someone they once loved. My mother says, Oh dear. In the afternoon she is unanimated. She gets a sponge from the kitchen. Then, bending to mop, she moves her hair from her face, and her hair turns auburn. The window rattles with a gust of wind, and her hair turns suddenly, uncontrollably, grey. Her dress is yellow. She sees her reflection in the sliding glass door imposed above an ant mound, ants move slowly along the dirt. She drops her face into her ink hands, descending.

The air is hot and laden in the desert suburb. There is no sense in representing the desert realistically when artificial water is everywhere, underground sprinklers hissing. The windows hallucinate in a wet mirage. Cement and hair spray dreaming, car wash, air conditioner, sweaty moon.

There is music from the speakers in the study, and this is the only indication of my father's presence. He loves opera and disappears inside it darkly. He loves tragedy. Mother's head is in her aging hands, two red thumb prints on her pulsing temples, touched, changing her brain waves locally, vodka, coyote, she screams in the kitchen banging sponges. Idiot-child! she curses me when her drunkenness has gotten mean. You peed on the carpet and the ink won't wash off! You are killing me, littttttle BAssstaAARD!

Monkey lady bangs pots all night, I whispered.

She was going mad. I would never know why. I could only conjecture her past. I was still so small I could not fly yet and I was frightened to death of my mother. I lay in bed, the white starched sheets still unwarmed by my flesh, my pelvis rose in the black, white thighs in my dreams. I will learn to fly, I say, folding my wings around me. Strait-jacket mutation, new life began with a collection of longings.

In the morning, I turn nine, a numerical complexity at last. I cut two masks out of construction paper, a mother mask and a daughter mask — similar faces, different sizes. Carefully slice the paper's edge into strips of hair that are separate from the cheek bones. Attach one mask to my own face, the other mask to my mother's face, allowing her lit cigarette to burn the only hole. Like the Greeks. Now do the vacuuming, I will do the sucking sound, I told her.

suck   MBret *sunaff* juice   Gk *hyei* it is raining   Lith *sunkti* ooze

The dictionary added:

examples of: sucked food particles from the tongue, sucked the membrane from the throat, using a tube (Fisbein) / the bee that sucks from mountain heath her honey (Wordsworth) / a vacuum pump sucks the steam out of the cloth (Von Bergen & Mauersberger) / was nearly sucked under by a bog (Brit. Bk News)/ the pull of gravity would suck the blood away from his head (Michener) / the sun sucked up the rain (Merillat) / thy valiantness was mine, thou suck'st it from me (Shakespeare) / sucked away their specie reserves (Morison and Commager) / the bemused spinster sucking culture from galleries (Canby) / sucking strength all round for the savage struggle (O'Flaherty) / suck me yes oh suck hard you bitch baby oh yes suck suck (John Holmes, Deep Throat) / all of us have been sucked out of our native soil and scattered in every unlikely corner of the world (Howard) / suck out the trachea (Koontz) / several centuries of essentialist thought have sucked dry reality (Modern Schoolman) / a child at suck.

father

Father was raised by a wet nurse because his own mother claimed to be a virgin, substantiating her claim by her lack of milk. My descriptions of my father will be few, but he stands always in the threshold of every room. My mother's eyes are everywhere. My mother's eyes in the family samovar. My mother's eyes in the sliding glass door. My mother's eyes in the antique toilette. My mother's eyes in the little plastic toilet mirror. My mother's eyes in the tumbler. Tonight, my mother is reflected and wedged. Father worries about her. Father makes symbolic and silent efforts toward meaning and love. He spins a vinyl on the old machine. Unable to recall that Mother hates opera, he plays her *La Traviatta* which he heard in Italy during the war, in a good time. He sits in his armchair, shrouded by music. Above him there hangs a wedding kimono which he bought in Tokyo after the war. On the kimono he sees peacocks of luck and blinks.

Now he looks into my bedroom and inclines his bald head. I have wept too loudly and attracted attention. Most nights, the moon and the pillow are equivalent and white enough to dry my eyes. My father comes to me. He holds a square white piece of paper in his careful hands. He smiles. Folds it in half, then in half again, then this edge, and the next edge, and the next, smally, and the next, more smally, and the next, Daddy, the paper, diminishing, into a bird.

our house of card and mirrors. overcoming gravity, or not. reflecting. our little house like a chinese box inside box inside. closed sequences.

mother and autumn

Mother sits at her desk. I can continue to watch her through the glass sliding doors if I wish to. See her mark and (now the practice of several s's) look up. I smile through the glass at her. I wave my origami birds, words on their wings, and paint pot in her direction. Reveal my red fingertips, ribbon splash on the garden dirt.

You're in the garden again. Yes. What are you doing? Writingpainting. She hates my writing, because it is unreadable, illegible, never fits between the lines, and when it's done I shred or fold it. I don't like to keep things as things or just things. Mother says, You don't know the difference between pictures and ideas. Let me teach you. Use a pen like a normal child. Dip a fountain pen in the underground springs in the desert, ink runs out, everything scribbled with movement. Horizon on my bitten fingernails, I could touch the view, scratch my veins with words. Use needles for precision. Has someone been talking to you about drugs? No. Pine trees. The sky opens dreaming. Have you ever heard of Dakinni-writing, Mommy? The Tibetan Buddhists say that only the Holy can read the clouds. And the Navajo — where do you learn these things? she asks.

The Salt River Indian Res. and the Gila River Indian Res. and the Papago Indian Res. and San Xavier Indian Res. and Fort Apache Indian Res. and Colorado River Indian Res. surround the city of Phoenix. How many thousand native Americans live here? A Navajo named HP was the cook in our school, but he left and became the cook in our prison. In school they called him HP sauce, and they thought that was really funny. HP was beautiful, long hair in a red ribbon and homosexual. Albinos and homosexuals are blessings to Navajo mothers. That is all that I know about the Navajo. And winos on Van Buren Street. And winos by the Amtrak station. The highways are flanked with shawled women selling necklaces or sheep skins.

Sometimes I write on my skin and this enrages my mother. Or I write on my outgrown clothes, paint them in words and cut up the cloth in little ribbons to bind my orange hair. On these rib-

bons, I write descriptions of myself. This enrages her further.
You're a narcissist/anarchist/kiss. Don't you know the meaning
of anything? At ten years old! She knocks on the window. Is
your room clean?

> Ours will pass this way, or in silence.
> Spelling, she says. Your spelling is lousy.

We are Mother and Daughter. See Mother watch herself in a
vague reflection of the sliding glass door, superimposed on the
garden. She moves her grey hair behind her ears, tucks her silver
pen behind her ears, clip-on earrings neatly. She shakes her
head at me. Will you play Mother May I? I ask. See her rise
toward me. Yes. No. Simon Says. No, she's going to use the toilet. I am laughing. It's not funny. Bodily functions aren't funny.
Hear a hum in the bathroom. It's just the fan, it's not her voice.
Behind the hanging towels, she falls asleep on the toilet. I don't
know why. Her cigarette runs out. Ashes on the plunger.
Eventually, I understand what has happened to my mother and I
walk quickly to the bathroom and wake her. Mommy, I say.
Ball-eyed, she looks at her shit scornfully. Marks its pale loose-
ness. Flushes. I look through something damp like hope, a
change of mechanical air in the filtered interiors, lint catchers,
flies on the inside screen.

dead bees

I want to leap this story forward in bare light autumn, because light in the desert resists measurement. Space opens up, I am allowed air in. Out in the autumn garden, I search for rotting flora. No apples to fall here, but the lemons continue swelling while the olives in gethsemane corrode, but not just now. The seasons in the desert move too purposefully for the luxury of decay, like the novel that leaves so much out and stops so cleanly at death.

Mother will not die. But the word *mother*, a vibration moving round a frenzy, humming bird and night bloom, will die. She will be sucked inward by desire. Mother longs for enclosure. Mother has stopped brushing her hair. Mother is so ugly. Mother sits at her desk, chewing pen stubs, eraser nibs, slips her fingers into the tangles of grey hair. Her fingers disappear, in knots consumed. For hours she will sit, one hand on her pen, the other in her hair, her unpolished nails sucked under. She is almost satisfied. She is somewhere unknown.

In the glass door she watches her reflection, to be certain it does not move and surprise the birds eating crumbs in the dirt. How do I understand? I understand that something is completed. I understand that when my mother buries her fingers in her hair, she is inside. She feels like she is one thing, although composed of many thousand strands. In her knot and her reflection she feels alone, at peace, and nowhere else.

When father comes home wheezing, his arms full of the groceries, mother does not answer the bell. At the front door, balancing the load of individually wrapped foodstuffs on his diminutive hips, father scrambles for his keys, and drops them in the drain, beneath the down pipe, amongst the season's rot. His fingers come up stinking.

Mother stands up and walks to the kitchen. The telephone is ringing. There are four million listings in our phone book, one million Phoenix numbers belonging to Fundamentalist

Christians rising from the Protestant ashes, 112 pizza joints, 48 Smiths, and I am eleven years old. Time is passing and I have become aware of its slight texture. My mother hated the desert and its millions of creatures. Outside there are hundreds of millions of things! she screams into the receiver.

1) gila woodpecker, red headed with black and white striped wings, shrieking. 2) quail. 3) the flycatcher sings at evening. 4) mockingbird. 5) crissal thrasher. 6) bees. Scavenger is responsible for bees. One day, bees attacked the eagles' nest in the sky, and the eagles, being short-sighted and having large beaks, were helpless. Scavenger, being human, killed the bees between his large brown hands and dropped two bee children through the sky hole, alive. As a result, there are bees on earth. And if you listen closely they will sing you their origins. 7) wind. I include wind as a creature because it feels and speaks. Aside from air in various motion carrying innumerable pollens and small viruses, there are several other dictionary meanings of the word wind: a destructive force or influence, a breath, something that is insubstantial, nothing, and the wind loves as I do. 8) ants. In the desert there are many kinds of ants. There are basic ants, looking taller than usual at noon because they are running on their hind legs to reduce contact with the burning ground. There are honey ants, gorged like jellyfish, hanging from the underground ceilings and feeding on themselves. Leaf-cutter ants dragging leaves to be regurgitated as fertilizer for their fungus nests. Velvet ants, who are really mutillid wasps, an inch long and brilliantly covered with hair, searching out a bees' nest in which to lay eggs. When the multitude of babies hatch, the young wasps will eat the larvae of their host. 9) scorpions and whip-tailed scorpions who are not scorpions, being huge and poisonless like dreams of monsters. 10) tarantula with irritating hairs, working its way into a woman's scalp and, there, having babies in a beehive as reported in the newspapers in 1970. 11) tarantula-hawk, not a hawk but a wasp, orange wings, blue body, which will stun the tarantula and drag it to a nest where the tarantula-hawk will lay eggs upon the paralyzed spider. When the eggs hatch, the young wasps will eat the body of their host. 12) More than 1,800 winged ants in the stomach of one nighthawk at any given moment. 13) etc.

My mother hated the desert because the more alive a thing was the more she feared it.

the dead

Now my grandmother's ghost walks towards me. She walks over
Black Mountain. She walks on a shallow cliff known as the pass
of the dead. My grandmother walks in refuse: coke cans, camel
butts, condoms, bones, dolls, stories, what we cannot say about
where we came from. Her body is incorruptible. She walks into
my breast.

history

She was lifting up her skirts, her bare hide feet, russet and horny, stinking of turf smoke, old baby shit and muck pig, her hands scaled by the stiff udders of a cow that gave nothing but dew, delicate and tasteless, till she killed it, and the calf and the pig and the hens, too. She had slaughtered her last lamb, and seven children were buried, conceived on seven nights over seven years while the chickens shook the rafters with shitty tail-feathers and the rooster cracked and squalled and humped and the pigs and piglets spewed and grunted beneath the bed and one by one her limby children witnessed her silently press in another child and another child with half-closed eyes and open legs beneath the sheets, torn between howling baby and begging cock, in a one-room cabin made of mud, body splitting every time. And no longer. Now she is leaving. She leaves chicken bones and babyclothes behind her. She is lifting up her black hem. White lips. Crystalled sweat marks in her armpits. Ties a bonnet. Smells the salt coast, the boats swollen wide in a surplus of death, exporting bodies to America. She will follow her ancestors who, under Cromwell, were shipped to New England as slaves, herded out of the Dublin ghettos, and forced onto sailing ships. She will take the ship to New York, and join the ancestral ghosts, pass through the garden gate and leave the fertile land. She will stop to beat a mule that she ate months ago, his pile of bones in the weed. She curses the bones by a useless God, turns her cross upside down, but she cannot remember the spell. Too many unnamed days have passed and she has forgotten witchcraft. Too many nights and she no longer cries. She ate her crying. God fed her tears as though she were a glutted child. He pried her mouth with his fist and tortured her with crying, the way rice swells with water in a stomach. And now she is leaving His territory, hay feeding the butterflies in the field where the dung pile seeped its wealth away in ditches, sinking cow pat, mule pie, chicken plucked stools, filthy and warm inside the earth, drained off down the mass-path toward the sanctity of one hundred new corpses and her seven dead children emitting gas. Richness. This was the Great Famine. So much will grow here. The oaks are thick and edible with caterpillars. She snatches one from a leaf. Swallows. See how she stumbles out the gate, drunk on water, hearing voices. Whose?

the dead

My mother walks beneath the cliffs, alone and drunk at night, calling curses up to the eagle's nest. Eagle feathers floating down upon her, my mother tears at her stinging flesh. Tarantulas are in her hair. Condor body parts are at her feet, condor wings that have been made into flutes, condor eyes that have been roasted on fires and eaten to sharpen human eyesight, condor quills that make very good cigarette holders. When my mother screams, her torso breaks cleanly in two, and, suddenly, these words fall out.

(unreadable)

history

This is the desert, night, the city, my childhood and barren, so I will take this timelessness and solitude to grave rob. Open the casket, enter the carcass, autopsy the patient. Something killed it, and I am assigned to discover what that was. Breathe on it with love, if you can remember that I loved my mother, loved my father, though you will not hear much that is true about him or her. If you are afraid of my parents, you can suck on American peppermint, for the Navajo say that peppermint will exorcise ghosts. And ghosts, the Navajo say, are the witches of the dead who behave much like the witches of the living: they dig up a body, blow on it to shrink it, put it in a pocket, bring it home, and sing to make it grow again. From these corpses, witches learn to control their world. And, for good or evil, this necromancy is similar to what the writer does: picking words dead from the dictionary, and arranging them prayerfully.

the dead

They gather, hundreds of them, like small winds, like clouds, like gnats, like geese, like city lights. One ghost meets another ghost, and they were family during life, so the one ghost kisses the other ghost in recognition, and suddenly I choke. There is a terrible stench in the air. One ghost bites off the other's tongue, because ghosts cannot love each other. My mother screams, over gin over ice, over the birdbath's reflection of the moon. In the mountains, hear the echo. In the swimming pool, waves. In the tumbler, see her face broken. This is what I witnessed nightly when cornbeetle calls looo lololo, coyote and owl call heya hey hey yeh oheya. But now I cannot hear them, because Carmen sings her own name on my father's stereo, and my mother screams, drunk.

father, mother and
the creatures of the water

At night, my father listened to opera. Sound. No body. His presence like a gap in the architecture, something overlooked in the plans, a small crack. He was always standing in the thresholds. A desk drawer waiting. A bookmark. The sleeve of a vinyl record in his hand. Having no contents, I filled him inwards with my imagination. He told no stories, and so I am left with scraps of my father, his history inferred by inlays on cutlery and the initials of my need like cut glass. His sophistication marred him in true space. It is through his awkwardness that I piece together his beauty.

To me, his childhood is entirely lit by candles in glass cylinders, sounding like hornets in captivity, reverberant. It is what I have captured about him with the faintest air supply. He was raised in a manor house on the crest of a hamlet. Always more English than Irish, he was rich and neglected. As a lone child, he never dined with his parents, but dined instead in the livery, with the shadows, and the servants coming and going with unwanted pity toward his unwanted body till their weak smiles cracked him like sunlight on veneer. His mother would have one believe her a virgin. His mother maintained her virginity in her absence of warmth.

My father is a man of expressionless light. Opera. Origami. Silence is a social grace. In the living room, my father moves like thin materials over airless windows. He told me once that Wheevle the butler — yes, he smiled, an unusual name, took him in his powdered hands and taught him the waltz. My father keeps three-four time and three-two time. I assume the rest. I have seen my parents dancing on happy days before the madness.

In my room, I imagine my father's nursery, his pressed tin model of an Hispana-Suissa, his black-buckled red-coats in formation on the bookshelf, and Macbeth, the first grown-up story in the nursery. Who was not of woman born and when Great Birnan wood to Dunsinane hill shall come. I imagine my father, like me, was susceptible to fiction, and riddles and lies. I imagine, after reading Macbeth, he listened close to the beech tree that touched the nursery window in night wind. Heard warnings. He ran. And when the soldiers grabbed him and dragged him to the gallows of Great Birnan, and hung him briefly so his screams snagged in the choke, and cut him down, and sliced him open so that his small torso belched from the gut and dinner fell out black on the scaffold, he woke crying.

I wanted to catch his tears.

It is night, and my mother is screaming at my father. She hates opera. My parents divide the house loudly. Father never says a word in defence, his language only through Caruso. Mother never says a true word, unreferenced, she roars pure sound, lost consonants in booze. She falls over her faces screeching names that have no persons. That woman! she barks. That man! Then, you don't love me anymore. Sometimes I wish she would die.

This is how it happened for father.

When my father was a child, he never saw his mother on normal days or nights, but one very early morning, he was summoned between two oak doors into the panelled bedroom. Surprised to see yellow lights around her head, and how blue her nightgown, blond hair, perfect cellophane skin, the myth of his mother's virginity was completing. Under hot-pressed sheets, his mother lay in white, the whiff of curdled milk and child's piss. Yes, that was one thing wrong with holiness.

Father stood before his mother feeling shamed, as if he had done that smelly thing to her. And yet he had never touched his mother's flesh except the brief moment he rubbed up against her vulva and fell into the cradle. Now he crossed his hands. Wore a new blue suit and a clean collar. Sweated. His mother did not look at him. Perhaps she was watching something crawl on the ceiling. He looked up, saw nothing, heard shadows. It was raining outside. He had to pee and thought of the Sahara Desert as his nanny had taught him to do in emergencies. He didn't move. His mother's jaw was hinged like a coffin and it was hard for her to make words. He waited. She said she wanted to tell him before she was dead that she had always been a virgin. The doctor broke my hymen at your awful birth. Now, she choked up phlegm, and a nurse caught it in a glass container. This soft yellow excretion, like a miscarriage, from her lips.

He pinched her words between his little fingers, and put them inside his torso. I can still see these words at certain angles, in certain pauses. But now, suddenly, none of this mattered because his mother died with a great commotion, maids' streamers flapping and long black tails of doctors. A bell rang. Large male hands shoved him to the side of the room, splintered into tudor panelling. His eyes lost his mother's face and were watching the ceiling, devils descending from the cornice, like hornets moving in jelly.

At the end of Carmen, silence rose out of father's armchair and mother's white mouth, froth. There was a gap which was truly night-time. I have heard that the ancient Irish worshipped everything that sang: mountains, ben of song, hills, sliabh of song, rocks, cloagh of song, lakes, lough of song, island, innis of song, bogs, cork of song, land, curragh of song, rivers, anagh of song, field, agh of song. Field means enclosed land. It also means battleground. There are many kinds of battles. The Norman conquerors came and then the Anglo-Saxon land owners came to England's Plantation of Ireland. They came like a new blockbuster to Topeka, Kansas, and suddenly the world changed, and the song stopped. Be quiet and you may hear the olives ripen and the blow-up dinosaur sink in the pool with a low hiss. The oranges and the lemons swell. Father walking slowly about the house, creaking floorboards. The loud opening and closing of cupboards. This was night, and like all the animals in the coolness, Mother was looking for drink. Father watched with one closed eye. Mother reeled in the linoleum squares of the kitchen, vodka and orange juice in a watery grip. There were no laws in the house, only music in the universe. A pause in my mother's mind. A lull in the wind.

The music stopped. It was summer. The window closed. Outside a great electrical storm touched down, headlines and the world news in father's hands as he relaxed over disaster. He sat back in his armchair, adjusting the matching arm doilies. Dinner consumed, with blood in his stomach, he was cold though the air was hot. Mother stood in the kitchen, drunk but longing to wash dishes. She was mobilized. Father said nothing. He read.

Mother washed a silver fish knife, bone handle, part of father's interminable inheritance like everything else my parents owned that was old and classy and oppressive. Mother complained as she washed how her ancestors had suffered, starved in the famine, fled to America, eating thorns. Father nodded. He had his own myths and now he had the paper. Flooding in the Philippines, the primaries, napalm.

Mother hated the fish knife. It was the first time in her life that she displayed her hatred of the fish knife. At the kitchen sink, mother ran the green scourer down the fish knife and over it, down it and over it, watching the silver scratch down the fish knife. Just yesterday, she asked me if I was mad, using the scourer. Always use the sponge. I should know better. Silver is money. Are we made of what? Money, I said. Do as I say, she whispered. But tonight, she was doing it herself with the scourer.

She ran the scourer down the fish knife and over it, harder, harder, something amiss in her fingertips, in the jilt of her neck, like a cat bit suddenly and the camera tilted, her body flayed. She scoured the fish knife harder, fiercer; a call jeered from her lips in fluorescent lighting, piercing the wallpaper, maybe coming from the neighbours, not her, not her, but I know it was she who stretched out her arms, stretching out across nations, each motion, like her red hair and grey hair that merged when she thrashed or rocked or snarled, while another voice rose out of her dead full belly and thundered, Are you mad? The scourer!

No, perhaps she said nothing except her body, this silent film.

I stand watching. And the world news is flipping pages on the wind, electrical storm touching down. Somewhere outside, a tree was on fire, burnt to the rhythm. Down it and over it harder until her fingers' knife point scraped the walls and carved the wounds into the paper Christ that hung above the cooker, and I think it too was burning. I watched as my mother tore through the wallpaper so that strips of little white men fell in strips of brainwaves from her body. My father jumped up from his arm-chair in loose trousers. Some seizures are induced by alcohol.

And yet the nurse said, chart and pencil in her careful hand: Some of the most beautiful brainwaves I've ever seen have come from the most disturbed people.

Mother shouted, her mouth black, her hair greased with con-ductive gel, electrodes like orphan's fingers: What do you mean beautiful?

And so the nurse answered: Clear, firm, perfectly normal lines. And some of the ugliest from people who show no signs of malfunction.

Electrodes are attached to standard areas. The electroencephalogram (EEG) amplifies and records the electrical activity of the brain as waves on moving strips of paper: alpha, beta, theta, delta. My mother was producing delta waves during the waking state, 2.5 to 3.5 cycles per second. This is abnormal. Delta waves only occur in young children and during deep, deep sleep.

After the screaming, my mother slipped down the glass sliding door, gasped on the carpet, blacked out. Lightning struck in the distance. Let me sculpt her from invisible pressed white sheets of forthcoming hospital beds that would hold her. Unformed, her form emerging from itself, from something else, from both, from neither, or not emerging at all, just being, but in all ways, incomplete and abnormal. In motion, breathing the shape of herself, she rises, falls. Her twisted spine, aching torso up the back, up the bodice, space between breasts, not the breasts themselves, her neck unfolds. But her head continues to sleep, dream, and forget its dreams darkly, as the body rises, hating itself, not knowing it is a body except by pain. This is what I understood: Mother hated herself. And her incomplete foot not yet in full motion, testing its muscles, serpents. Her body arising up to the arteries, across the lip tremor, the black retina motion, the forehead greased to the dream that rises in empty space, and the glimpse of nurses, readers, the dream becoming the nurses, the readers, monsters they are all monsters, venom, scorpion, daughter, buzzard can you hear the buzzard? she asked me when she woke, whhzzzz, in her mind, sky, becoming writing on white strips of paper, as if the waves were siphoned off the sea.

When the momentum was spent, my mother's brain returned slowly, stopping in time again. Just breathing. Often at night she was to lie on the floor, crumpled and breathing. Catching her mind back into her body like a flying fish. My father, who would become accustomed, placed the fish knife in the drying rack, washed a spoon. And in the spoon, in my mind, there was the wind. How it moves over the water.

My mother was like a great sea, roaring, that I would pass over. I would pass over her, as my mother's mothers had passed over the Atlantic, had landed on Ellis Island, had passed over the Brooklyn slums, the flat lands of Ohio, turnips, Iowa, stopping for breath and all those potatoes that no one will ever visit, Kansas, and down to the tip of oh-godly and interminable Texas, over the purgatorial miles of America, bashing bibles, harvesting crop, over all those words of truth, passing, like the wind tonight that has come a great distance to love me. My grandmother, or one of my grandmothers, would arrive in the Arizona desert to make a new life and raise a child. Her people would kill many better people when they arrived.

history

Snow on the mountains, still coming white. 1863, the Apache and the Navajo had not yet been thoroughly conquered, but the Spanish had given way to the more meticulous Americans. That year, my grandmother came West in Victorian gear with shears, beads, spoons, knives and barcelona kerchiefs, kettles and buttons, a new baby and master. This was trade, brass button fixed on a Navajo's sash. And guns. This was war. Said General Carlton to the Navajo tribe, calling on the practical and biblical at once, We will hunt you like wolves; this war shall be pursued against you until you cease to exist or move. Don't breathe. The Navajo lived fireless on pinion berries, too smart to make smoke. No clouds, no words, no whisper, no salt. That winter, sheep froze in the dunes, spring, cicadas burnt in their stalks. United States Scorched Earth Policy. The Navajo hid in the highlands and canyons, lit no fires, went out with no sheep, drank only in rock basins filled with rain water. Holed up, Daddyo, makin' room for Sweet Unc Sammy while in an outpost of Flagstaff, some pockmarked, ruddy-faced immigrant (nickname: Bad Red) played a fanfare outside his clapboard house, new wife looking on, last wife abandoned on the Donegal coast of Northwest Eire with five kids and a donkey in the peat. Heeeee-haw. And now Bad Red had his big house and his new chick in the desert. His big house would burn seven times before he died at thirty of the pox, but today he was happy. His trumpet pulled on the cliffs, like a man on a goatee: there was a landslide and Kit Carson came of age, aiming at the leftest most leaf on the old poplar tree... bang. This ere America now! said Bad Red. Purdy! This desert ere America now! Now it gotta name, buddy. What it called before? my grandmother asked her new husband. ... Jus ugly ... On the cliffs a strange noise sounded. Jericho with no walls to break down. And coyote: heya hey hey yeh oheya.

ravens

When my mother screamed and washed the air with her fury, it was hard to believe that our family had arrived anywhere at all. It was hard to believe we had not been sucked under by the sea, into the mouth of some great belching whale. We are its feed, its catch. Time tasted like lousy flesh. Already my mother had swallowed the small fish carcass. She had eaten many bloody things in one bite, and maggots were the first ingredient of her curses. In her body, I imagined like met like, and both being filthy, following the pattern of all creatures who do not love, the likenesses waged war and would destroy each other.

As Mother and Beniamino Gigli competed howls up the stairwell, I ran to my room and covered my ears. I looked up Scream in the dictionary. **Scream** / OE hraefn — more at Raven / I turned the pages backwards to R...

Out the window I could see a high-rise, and on the twenty-fifth balcony a shrunken figure with a giant broom carried the dust to sky. I wanted the human to jump. They are heroes who get to the sky. Look up, look down, breathe shit from the city. In an alley a beggar eats his thumbs, his skin swimming like heat mirage, head to toe in lice. In summer the rats come up through the broken manhole. The shopping district lulls and profit falls to the overhead of the air conditioner. Leisured women tie chiffon blouses around prominent ribs in the windless heat and drink saccharine coffee beneath red umbrellas. The city burns. The desert rats are thirsty, come looking for puddles of urine.

Tonight, on a park bench, a woman nurses. I see her from a graceful distance in the small city park with the fish-mouth fountain, her fingers moving slowly around her breast. Her head bent in a gentle ecstasy. Look closer. In fact she is painting her fingernails silver. And a man stops in a Corvette, opens the passenger door. She raises her body from the crux of her vulva. Her red heels. Wet nails. To the metal door. He revs. Blows gas.

Kisses. Enter. Highway and away to a sweating morning. And now, on a park bench, an old man cries over a postcard.

raven /OE hraefn; akin to Skt krpate he laments, implores.

When my parents think I'm sleeping, I open the dress-up trunk and tie on my grandmother's bonnet. Shhh. In a black bonnet, I bend my head and enter the past. I play at being my grandmother, crossing the Atlantic, she is passing over, and downstairs, opera.

aria

In a black bonnet, she bent her head and exited the past. She entered into the hinder part of an enormous vessel and passed, departed thence, amongst thousands of Irish others, their emaciated bodies. They stunk. They swayed with lice. The ship heaved off from its ropes and chains and sickled anchor, heavier than the sand of the sea or the whale itself, dragged off from the coasts as the waves beat over. With wind the sea covered the bastions, and the thousand heads inclined hullward beneath pounding waters of the sea on the bulwark skull like a brutal baptism. The sea and all that is in it, the black rider that has been thrown into the sea by spirits, host-become-flesh cast into the sea by protestants, priest washed into the sea, twelve oxen and thirteen cows that fell over the cliff into the sea, and swine cast down by Christ, and fishers of years that fished and drowned in the sea, its broken dominion is flung upon their heads. Corpses and waves and the fish of the sea be gathered together, and is flung upon their heads.

See her standing in urinated shifts. Open her mouth. Without bread and wine, a priest gives the eucharist. Breathe the veil of salt and coal as a stranger sweats down my grandmother's bodice. Peel black cotton from her breasts, wet fingernails of clay beneath their folds. We are standing, leaning into the wave.

One thousand of us squat, and piss, and urine rolling stale and dry across rough, tilted floors. All human excrement feeds the ship rats tonight. Dig in the shit for something voided whole, and eat it again. Like something congealed in the heart of the sea, like something rotten, the floating casket rocks and wails. Hear wave beat on a vile of sound, the laboured grey hull in which foreignized creatures keen low mulled tones, gasp breath high, sing my bonnie, wretch, swoon, slobber, sleep vertical, cough up slugs of blood, smack children, comfort one another, pray loudly. Schizophrenia in a crowded skin, wailing discordant stories, vomiting identically within hands reach of each other's strangulation. Here is the urge to kill when you cannot breathe enough. Babies scream. Divide air between a thousand. Push sweating bodies back to standing. As if each one of these starved beings were a mangy and forgotten Christ stood seasick upon the waves, the waves reared beneath them, send them forth, oh Lord, in a grace of wind.

all lull in the squall

It is quiet downstairs. I lean over the banister in the black bonnet, sliding. lull: lullaby / a temporary cessation or lessening of the wind or storm / a period of intensified quiet / a relaxed or dazed state of mind / a tube through which blubber is passed to tubs in the hold of a whaling ship. Mother has collapsed by the sliding glass door. Summer opens to the garden night, night azalea, night cholla. But I never believed there was an outside. Electricity, like city walls, enclosed our house in the orange dark though sometimes a cat or an insect came within. My mother's cheek on the hot glass, drunk. She slept with her lids peeled open, and in the morning her eyeballs were dry, exposed to the wind all night.

Cicadas scream. And on Ellis Island, my grandmother signs her x in a large book, wherever the finger points her, in a world of black and white photographs and dust. She loses her name and enters altered, amongst altered thousands, like the insane called out of the pits of Jerusalem. Her reflection in every shop window. Superimpose herself now, like an experimental photographer, above an advertisement for soap. She is filthy, she murmurs. She is filthy. She is filthy. She has never seen so many images of her face so many times. mirror: [L. mirari to wonder at] a polished or smooth substance that forms images by the reflection of light / something in which a true image may be visualized / something exemplary that may serve as a model / the speculum of a bird's wing / with mirrors: by or as if by magic.

I untie the bonnet and place it back in the chest. I return to my age and my flowered nightgown, and I go to bed. But I am not done with this game, I will never be done with such games. There will be nights in childhood when I can see the wind, a view through the sand so far as the cliffs of death, so far as where desert meets ocean. A mirage that I will leap across. I would learn to fly.

On those nights the past is visible and history comes like

dawn, quick, look away for a moment, look back, someone is absent. They have left small evidence: handprints of the wind. Be quiet, you in the desert. And below the screams of cicadas and revving engines on a Saturday night, hear the flycatcher. Sleep.

list of song titles the Irish Druid's sang: [sing them all in monotone]
Dark Dark Destructions, Dark Dark Massacres, Dark Battles, Invasions, Sieges, Pillages, Raids of Dark Cattle, Rapes of Dark Women, Dark Loves, Marriages, Exiles, Navigations of Dark Places, Marches, Voyages to Dark Lands, Dark Grottoes, Dark Visions, Pomps, Tragedies. / **addendum:** Dark Swoons, Dark Confessions, Dark Lies, Empty Hours, Endless Idles, Drugs, Anger, Dark Insomnia.

dream at the age of thirteen

I dreamt a black cat entered through the doors to what is not the outside. It may have been born in the house, and yet no one had noticed it growing. Moon on the tip of its tail, words stung, caught in its teeth, and did not articulate. The cat said nothing, being a cat in heat who is only heard to screech. Cats cannot desire without violence, so it remained kindly silent. It licked the kitchen floor in front of the stove where my mother's bare feet had hottened. It tasted my mother's bacteria on the linoleum, and then it deposited a small pool of vomit.

It walked the corridors to what was called the vault. Instead of a basement, our house had only a crawl space that flooded yearly, the inside walls running with condensation where heat wept against cool nights but could not come out. Although the vault was shallow, and descended only beneath the back porch, tonight it descended deeper. The walls blackened, and the ground flowed. And the cat and I walked inside.

Fluid earth. This is what we saw: slush, where rock is near melting point; slurry, moving water on a sheet of sediment; solidified lava hardened and cooled into solid ripples that resemble a beach at low tide or stretch marks on my thigh preserved anciently, rounded troughs, crests breaking off, suncracks, mudflats, tidal reaches that time has dried and shrunk, forming a pattern of polygonal cracks. We walked between the cracks. Vegetation sunk to the bottom of a magma river. We walked over the river. Sediment crushed the plants below, the downwarping of land formed coal at the tread of our feet. This earth grew fire. Land burned into being, matter pouring up from the earth in lava like a lover's face beneath me, freezing in solitude, unadorned, vision of the sad that becomes stone.

Shale, sandstone, red marls, clay-impregnated limestone, slugs of salt, all climbed the walls like gaudy Victorian paper. A stalactite hung, like a chandelier, a slow dripping voice, no light to reflect within it. Great bells of hardshell clinging to the ceiling, fossils, secreting a brittle exterior cup of calcium carbonate. The footprint of a lynx climbing the walls of this prehistoric zoo. I ran my hands over a human handprint. Fossil of a frightened worm, an ammonite's coil, a fly preserved in amber, casts of teeth, tiny electronic cities of bismuth, tarnished bornite like the glistening blue bodies of fish and glamour ladies, the gentle snow and wave patterning of a thunder egg, and a setarious nodule like a businessman's brain. Lava burnt the rubber off my sneakers. Rubies blistered red inside a mundane igneous brown stone. And a geode like a cranial accident, broke cleanly.

All this was here in the vault and the cat and I were here, history is here. Scar tissue where a meteorite slammed into earth and disappeared, or attached, carbuncular, or came down at night slowly like an unseen angel looking for body. It is enough to be ugly, it is a body anyway, and many do not have them. Collision is union. Salt in the air dissolves history. Humanity. What million BC saw the liberation of hands from locomotion when we left behind swinging nimbly in childhood, threatening to become something by the work of our own hands? What is the date of this hand print on the wall? The hand is mutilated. One day its maker would turn pages looking for answers, looking for names. Call himself *homo habilis*. What million BC saw a double vault for total walking on the sole of the foot, but imperfect index finger and short thumb? This pre-human who walked like a human and like most humans was not human. He was the first recorded toolmaker and he could have been perfect, but he did not know how to love yet. His teeth, the most powerful set of chewing teeth ever known, were eventually sold in Chinese drugstores as belonging to dragons. Strangely, there is little tooth decay. Call himself Parnathropus. What million BC saw a child born with big strong toes, short and separate, the child a vegetarian, the child who opened seeds between molars, the child whose face bent with the weight of its own muscle which maybe did or did not develop the brain, or, on what does the soul grow? The child who slept beneath a tree and climbed it when scared or scared dreaming.

The cat instructed me. We stopped on a moss and emerald ledge. The cat said, Build me a grave. I built a rectangular structure to the cat's dimensions. I heard the cat's teeth sing, though it did not screech. Its small black mouth lifted slightly, though I could not say it smiled. I put my finger in its mouth. I thought of milk in my nipples. Its teeth clung to my finger and my finger dripped. I raised the cat into the hot damp air, lowered it into the enclosure. And I sealed it.

thirteen

Something about the shape of the wind that day, as it poured west a thousand miles from the flat and useful lands of origin. It had come a long way. There where it had whirled into being, begun somehow in the cracks of heat. Now the wind had abandoned its beginnings.

Now it had swept unhindered and virgin, over the sucking boredom of acres, thoughtless homestead, mechanised farmlands, totally predictable bend of a cornstalk beneath its seamless force, electrical wires trembling, phone wires trembling, connecting, and usefully connecting the death of an insecticized midge to the phone call home. Over the straight, hot asphalt lapped down flat for mile on silent mile, the car as the crow flies over the hours, over the time change west. Over and over the wind moved blackly, slowly and unnamedly.

And now there was something in the altered shape of the wind, now that it entered the ash lands, the barren lands, entered the hidden lands of the horribly present, entered here by grey passes of sunlight wedged between barb and weed and scorpion, entered here between a girl's white open mouth and red trailing hair, and dead volcanic mountains, distorting me. Here is the wind. It has come a great distance. Feel it on me. Feel me.

In its journey it has become something smiling and hideous, unrecognisable from genesis, ugly, contorted, a self-made deformity to be as proud of as a dream. See me.

the desert journal

history

It was spring when my grandmother made the journey west. She went by horse and coach and foot. She said it was endless, west. Flanks and ladies splattered, sweaty bridle, slathering horse, two pink fists and a stub-red chin on a rope, dragging the whole lot forward. Go forward, go forward like the children of Jerusalem! Get down and walk woman! a man shouted. There was silence behind cussing, and sloshing wheels on mire, and religious fervour over profit. Someone would be rich, this land. There was a drone in every head cutting hot silence, cold silence, whatever the season, the continuous past-noise and future-noise, regret, hope, tomb, house, scraping dirt and sky, and meanwhile, the present stunk. Too much water, no water.

Men's armpits like dungpiles, steaming turnips in summer, ice-box in winter, the pubic hairs fell off. Hysteria was being created in Europe for elegant women but it would take forty years to define itself analytically, and on the frontier who read books? Wombs rose and disturbed the blood supply or maybe it was just that goddamned corset. Take it off, the man smiled. Out here, bad behaviour meant bad weather and pull yourself together and forgive me, I'm pregnant. Out here there was no inside.

A woman hid her fair skin under a broad bonnet, frayed parasol, showers of black lace, and stepped down in the muck. My grandmother had cut peat in the bogs when her husband left her for America. The earth she knew grew fire. It was flammable for miles. Now, somewhere in the plains, she grabbed a stick, like a magician's staff, snake twisting with glycerine, and jammed it hard under the wheel, sunk to the waist. You could say she buried herself. Everywhere, immigrants, like small pagan standing stones scattered after Christ, stood bent every which way. The sky lay on them. Cloud trailing and carrying away the mind. Who'd know the desert flooded or froze? Where were the olive trees? Everywhere the land was drenched and frozen. No one but God's eye over a land that looks dead but isn't. Empty, uninhabited, but isn't.

My grandmother edged away from the others, space and
nowhere to hide. She thought of pissing. Made small efforts
toward modesty over and over westward. She dragged down her
linens and straddled. Small piss-river cutting and sudden descent
and red-brown earth, flat. Never seen rain like fury before.
Never seen so many stars, emptiness, ice, Indians, Mexicans. Just
shoot wild your own fear, hunger, hatred, stories, bigotries, there
was life and money at stake. In the coach she had a baby like the
screech-owl howling in the ambush, heat, cold, hell how she
hated it. But it was land and food. What the mind can get
attached to. There was wild game too, some you ate, some you
skinned, some you sent to the governor of Santa Fe for reward.
Stop doubting. There was enough rope to hang everyone who
disagreed with this beginning and still rope left over to lower
coffins of the falsely innocent and the truly innocent into grave-
yard, backyard, all of it sanctified by force.

Sure, monsoon and coyote could trespass on owned property,
but one day even nature would succumb to the coalition of mind
and fist, man the toolmaker, myth maker, making himself by his
own design, grid plan. Politicians dipping silver pens in ochre
ink, writing black railway sleepers across the mottled states.
Nature sanctioned out in plot and allotment. We own our
graves, Sir. We are in control of our lives. Nature will be curbed,
Mr. President. The world will blossom and pave. Asphalt. In the
future, they will make all asphalt from crushed glass.

the present

Walk beneath a linear sky, wonder who is up there? Walk in soft ash that slid down on a schoolhouse and buried the children alive. Who is down here between live volcanoes, flat ridges called mesas, and slagheap-like mountains called buttes? Who is low in the history of the earth slowly malleable in the hands of water or faith? Even in the dry winter, red mud falls singing from the cliffs that inevitably give way, leaving discarded heaps of earth like burial mounds, reminders of the last and furious spring, that mark a lost existence, while the Little Colorado charts time. Whose time? Whose existence?

I had left home. I was hitchhiking. I walked off the sidewalk on my thirteenth birthday. I had forsaken the route between the drugstore and my home. I knew how to roll the supermarket cart, how to develop film with my name and deposit, how to inflate the rubber dinosaur in the pool, how to come home for dinner when my mother screamed. I knew that I could not enter the past, but if God made the city bloom like the rose in chrome and palm trees, at least I could enter the desert and be rid of Him. My tongue turned white and adhered to my fillings.

A Navajo woman stopped in a Ford pick-up. She was driving down the white line. Her truck had a long scratch. Strange straight highway, look down the length of it. Tar snakes in the heat and is writing words. She pulled up beside me, rolled down her window, her face swollen with warmth, no creases. Where you goin? she asks. Nowhere, I reply. So I take you to a butcherin, she says. Tonight, she will take me to a sing.

We drove north onto the Navajo reservation. Breath coming up from the dash with the heat. Nothing out the window but road and rock, tumbleweed rolling like thought over stillness. Arroyos and stretchmarks. The Coca-Cola truck leaving empty from another delivery. Asphalt melting at noon and cooling hard by two a.m. A man and five kids fixing a flat on a beat-up white Chevy, a boy coiled over the spare, rolling head-first toward the concrete, crying, Look Dad. Gas station with a grey pump. This seat full of beer cans. I start counting, get to twenty-two. Push em on the floor by you feet, the driver tells me. Her plush skin. I take off my sneakers, glide my arches over the cylinders.

She points through the glass, my eyes follow like a tail. I call that Black Mowten, she says. (The rock walls crept, and a mongrel twitched in the nearby shade, playing dead and dreaming. I couldn't see for the glare.) She said, Guns an dreams carry us up Black Mowten. (At that time, I understood next to nothing that she said. My mind followed the paved road, journey on forever, if you want to, and nowhere to get to.) Monsters were killed here, she says, an when they died they left corpses of mowtens, ther blood still shakin earth.

Who were the monsters? I ask.

She smiles. Then she points at my face with her lips.

She stopped the truck dead, there was no shoulder. We climbed to a cliff where the images of several humans were carved in stone, a woman wearing a long skirt and large hat carrying a book and disintegrating, wedged free by ice, cut along the plains of weakness, dissolving in monsoon springs, like sugar in coffee, edges of the cliff rounding off. Erosion and it was happening to her face. I asked, what are they?

Picture rocks. Tells a story.

How old are they?

Old. They people are dead, but the rocks not dead. The rocks got the tongue of they people.

Is that a woman?

Priest never woman.

This here?

Priest boat.

That?

Gun.

These men lying sideways?
Indians.
This?
That the eagle who take the Indians to the sky.
One eagle lifts them all?
Ther light. Ther dead. It easy.

A black crow flew northward into the wind. A glowing blue
stain in the sky. A hawk attacked. A prairie dog rose dead into
the defunct air. A mongrel woke. Pigeon-toed and furious, a
badger. A solution of limestone, ground water and sweat dissolved in a subterranean spring. There was water somewhere.
But the desert was soaked in blue mirage. There was coffee, too.
An old man hailed us from his horse, his tongue shifting a leafy
tobacco gob in his left cheek. He clucked sheep away from his
horse hooves. Behind the flock, a swarm of nine brown women,
carrying knives. Behind the women there was a hogan. Hogan,
she said again. Home.

hogan

Feathers hang from the ceiling beside a leather pouch full of
yellow cornmeal, fake fruit, real corn cobs strung together
between wooden forks, and dried red peppers on a fish line. A
cracked mirror is nailed to the wall; on the warp, three eyes
shimmering. A basket decorated with a bead medallion is stuffed
with combs, earth-dyed wools, and whittled presses, the tools for
the loom which is only a bed frame stood vertical and strung one
hundred times in a double loop with half a blanket in the weaving. The Spanish once reported that Navajo blankets were tight
enough to transport water. Now a kerosene lamp lights a miniature saddle, a trophy from a rodeo, and a cowboy poster. Under
the bed, a collection of Women's Weekly bought at the
Mormon junk sale. A radio plays on batteries, tuned to the
WindowRock radio station featuring country jamborees and

Navajo song cycles, announcing local ceremonies, intertribal powwows, rodeos, and helicopter food drops when the dirt roads disappear in the snow. An advertisement requests a Navajo woman between thirty and fifty who doesn't drink and has absolutely no family responsibilities to take care of an elderly man. A smashed-up toilet stores canned foods, a pop-up toaster spouts dried flowers and a knobless television is powered by the battery of the pick-up truck outside. The hogan door slightly open to allow the cable through, wind enters, and in winter, it is freezing sound. Outside is the shit-hole. But inside is a bucket for waste water in the day and piss in the night when the temperatures drop too low, freezing genitals under no cloud cover. Ice chest, brown innards. One unit of a battered fitted kitchen, missing cupboard doors but the counters are clean. A grey, wet cloth smells of virus. This is one room. This is her whole house. There is a circular hole in the octagonal ceiling, and below it the central fire roars in an empty oil-can turned on its side. A metal cylinder punctures the can and carries the smoke out the smoke hole like a throat after trachaeotomy. Her plump brown wrists bedded with silver, she takes a tin can from the ice chest. She sharpens a boy scout knife against the oil barrel stove. A couple of upward heaves, gestures like pounding soil to open a can of corn, she dumps the kernels into a single bowl and calls me daughter.

Sun reaches down his yellow talons, scratches out my blue eyeballs.

butchering

In the yard, the butchered ewe hung from a dead tree. Dogs circled the carcass, teasing scraps. A crow flew away with sheep gut in its beak. A baby dragged full diapers between fat legs. Navajo babies drank coke. I vomited at the first incision as the sheep torso opened like an asshole. Spilling out. Women pointed at me and laughed. One held the brain in her hand, to be used later for tanning the hide. One held a garland of intestines to bind a basket drum. I drank coke too and sweated. And this woman driver, who will ask me to call her my desert mother, butchered like brushing her own hair.

The flock ate bad grass and eyed the red butchering, incapable of imagining their future. My desert mother stripped the bloody vomit shirt from my torso and gave me a velvet one. She said, you wear pants? and threw a skirt on my lap. The old shepherd clucked, slipped down from his horse, and gulped water from a tin cup. He tied a kerchief on his head, mounted, and rode away again bringing the sun down. The sheep in front of him became white stones and sparks.

the sing

The vehicle of song is the story and its intention is the healing. Medicine and religion are equivalent. The sing controls the supernatural forces of the world. Each song-ceremonial (the Night Chant, Bead Chant, Big Star Chant, Shooting Chant, Wind Chant, Enemy Way, Blessing Way, Flint Way, Hail Chant and Water Chant) features a different legend, hero, and the hero's patron gods. The adventures of the hero are recounted through a song cycle containing hundreds of songs and litanies. The patient identifies with the hero and absorbs the power of the gods, whereby balance (which is the cause of health) returns to the world and the one who is *sung over*.

A sing may last between five and nine nights (counted by nights not days). On the first night the hogan is blessed and power objects are touched to the patient's body. An upside-down basket becomes a dull drum, and the song cycle commences. The medicine man (there are medicine women in theory) presides over the ceremony with the help of assistants (family and tribal audience only; tourists are not welcome at these events). On the first day, prayers being made at dawn, a huge fire is laid in the hogan for sweating and application of emetics. Prayer sticks are stuffed full of jewels and feathers, and are lit (symbolically) by a large crystal held to the sun and then placed, burning, where the gods can view them. These prayer sticks are a compulsory invitation to the gods.

The actions of the first day are repeated on the second, third and fourth days. Each night the song is repeated in praise of a different deity as featured in the hero-story. On the fifth day, the medicine bundle is emptied and laid on the doorstep as a further invitation to the gods to be present at the making of the sand paintings, highly stylized illustrations of the story. Sand is coloured and filtered through the medicine man's fingers onto the hogan floor. The sandpainting is a temporal altar upon which the naked patient sits and is *sung over*, becoming the hero herself and gaining access to divine powers. Made and destroyed each day, the sandpainting is swept up and carried from the hogan, dispersed to the four directions. On the final day of a typical ceremony, the patient's body is painted. The patient has bathed in yucca suds and dried herself in cornmeal. The final night's sing extends until dawn when the patient *breathes in* the dawn. This way, she acknowledges the power of the gods upon her.

night chant

Night Chant is named for the dance of the masked gods.

Now it is dark and the crowds gather outside by a huge fire. A drunk grins and twists in the sand and, away from the light, becomes nothing. My desert mother spits. She stands, tall in her small body claiming space, arms squared, unmoving, no demonstration of warming herself, she stands as if one thing in this universe must happen at a time. She allays chaos. We wait outside for song in the hogan to commence. We have bought frybread and coffee for a dollar in a makeshift booth. She rolls a knot of starch around her tongue while birds open and close above her, or maybe bats beneath the antipodal stars. She spits on the ground again and covers the spit with dirt. Her toe.

You cup empty? she asks me. Give it to me. She spits in my coffee. I do not understand this, but it's okay because I am thirteen and I hate coffee. You gonna sing all night, she says, one hand on the styrofoam cup, the other drawing my hair from the neck of the blouse she has lent me. She sweeps the red strands behind my back. Red fire. I twirl a strand. Don't do that, she says, you lose some. She moves my arm to my side, spits in my cup. I'm tellin you what you gonna do in the hogan tonight. I nod. So listen. Yes. (I don't understand anything.) We all gonna sing with the medicine man, but you don't know the words, so you not gonna sing, an the gods gonna dance till mornin. Ther gonna dance, then ther gonna not dance. Then the sun gonna rise under the red curtain that over the door. The sun gonna pass by the grains of blue an yellow sand. The sun gonna pass into masks of the gods, an the gods gonna rise up tremblin. The sun gonna move into the one who been sung on, the patient. She only a little girl this time. An the song gonna make her holy by her gods, gonna make her well by her gods, an the sun gonna fill the hogan in the mornin, flood it. The masks of the gods'll breathe slow, be fed first like baby. Then, everyone eat. Yeh?

I nod blankly. A yellow glow one hundred miles off is a city sun. It is midnight, here is night, at least I know to call it that. I know I have never seen night before. In the desert, heat escapes from the earth into empty skies. Divide the heat with my white hands like phosphorescence in a placid sea.

She asks me, Cold? She tightens a blanket around my chest. She turns a phrase out of my language. Turn the heat up in the pick-up grandma, she says to a shuddering woman beside her. Go inside. A bow-legged granny purses her lips in agreement and exits, hauls herself into the Ford and slams the door. Everyone has arrived in pick-up trucks. They have parked perfectly. Metallic lines in empty space. Mudguards drag in the sand. The fire will leave scorch marks in the sand and emptiness beyond the perimeter of light. We are waiting. Her big hands.

She spits in my cup. What is it? She is aware of witches. She lists rules. (The occasional spark falls beyond this circle. One hundred guests moving in and out amongst the gods. She is aware of witches.) Never put scraps of food in the garbage, she says. Keep you spit, hair, whatever fall off you body. Even children an drunks know that. If you taste coffee, you in coffee. If you spit, you on the ground. Someone could pick you up like that, in spit, coffee. Could make you do what he want. (She whispers to me, knowing she shouldn't tell these things and that right-knowledge means to be holy, and she shouldn't whisper because whispering and silent prayer are two signs of witchcraft, and she is not alone now, she is in a crowd now, in the circle of the fire, the perimeters, where nothing should be broken, but she is breaking it. I do not know why. She is talking to a white girl about witchcraft, a white girl who might be powerful having wandered where the girl does not belong, unprotected and yet unharmed.) In a pot he put a live lizard an a couple of mice or rats, she whispers. When they die of thirst an starvation, he grind them up into pollen. Roll the pollen into a ball, an throw it at you. She spits. That how he do it.

Who does what?
She laughs loudly. Don't know, she says, though I think she does.

inside

As the crowds move toward the hogan, I see only the flicker of bright skirts and blankets and silver but mostly nothing human. It is too dark. Those who drift away, or wander toward their pick-ups, drink cheap wine in the cane break, kiss, fondle, whisper, are a solid darkness in the lesser dark of the unlit earth. At night in the desert, they disappear altogether, and when they return, before they step into the fire's circle, they appear only as density, a lingering trajectory of darkness, a black threshold, in which to fall deeply. This is what it means to be outside.

the blessing

I am a lucky girl. I think this woman is a bird. This is not a dream. Today, my school friends went to the mall.

the patient

For whom everyone has gathered. A young girl with fat cheeks sucked out from illness. In her prairie skirt and silver belt, velvet shirt, sweat marks, her mother's turquoise necklace, pink ribbon in her hair, she sits wrapped in a blanket, shivering in the hogan. She is waiting for us all. We bend our heads, and enter through the short, blanketed door. The frame is juniper wood, bedding of dry mud, shape octagonal. The door opens to the east where no evil can enter. The crowds enter and sit. Men in cowboy boots and cowboy hats, horned necklaces of turquoise and silver belt buckles, sprawl their wire flesh, crossed ankles, heals on their steel toes, laughing at each other. The women, in velveteen blouses and turquoise hair clips, sit upright, muttering quietly, more accustomed to waiting, less accustomed to heat, not trying to move. The patient waits in the west behind the fire, and does not look up. Her hair hangs over her face like a branch under snow. Tonight, she is a beautiful exile for her own protection. No one can touch her body without initiation, because the gods will come to dance for her tonight, and the song will be sung for her mind, for schizophrenia, blindness, epilepsy, or paralysis, which one? The gods will dance, exit, enter, dance, exit, enter, replicating the flickering retina, the jagged brainwaves, the fit, waves of fire in the centre of the earth. It is hot inside her belly from the fire. She is not well. Everything replicating the nature of God, the way interference in this world is sporadic. She breathes strangely. She is wrapped in a bright yellow pendleton blanket, patterned mountains reduced to geometrics, desert down to desert, heat stored in its hot colours and this grasp of life in its tight wool, the pattern readable. She is like me. The gods will come to heal her which means to bring her into a song which is a story, for song is always a story and the story is the sigh of the universe, and the sigh is the sound of the human who moves through her history saying her name and the gods listen. This is the wisdom of many tribes, but not of mine.

There was not enough oxygen in the hogan. I shifted my legs. Too many people. I stretched. My eyes blurred. My desert mother said my name. Once I heard my name said with kindness. I will not repeat it here. Suddenly the door opened on the desert night. Air. A god entered. My mind drifting. Air. What is mine?

The mind is everywhere. What is mine is the photocopied prep manual of the sleep-induced EEG, electrode paste in my drunk mother's hair. Things that flicker, says the game show. The tv after shutdown. Icecubes. Streetlamps losing contact. To get a positive reading, refrain from taking anti-convulsants, tranquilizers, barbituates, and other sedatives for forty eight hours before the test. That includes liquor. Are you mad? my mother screaming. We will determine epilepsy, diagnose intracranial lesions, evaluate electrical activity in metabolic disease, head injury, meningitis, encephalitis, mental retardation and psychological disorders, as well as confirm brain death. Avoid activities such as blinking, swallowing, talking, or other human movements for they will be recorded falsely as brainwaves.

god enters

With a whooping gate, a chicken-pecked blessing on the legs, heart, spine, shoulder, head, trail of his hand to travel out the mouth, the breath of the patient, the god leaps. The god grunts. His god-nose grows up his forehead into a painted cornstalk where a bird perches, between his square eyes, above his cowl of evergreen sprigs. He is masked. Halloween. I understand nothing.

Blue jeans give away his partially human status. Christ. A stomach hangs over his bones, his naked chest smeared with clay to keep the cold from his guts. But inside the hogan is hot, small, full and fills with song and I cannot translate pain or lyrics in a foreign tongue.

I lay my head on my desert mother's lap and the medicine man sings, leaning his fist on his jeans, squatting on one knee. Head drooped, he draws in the dirt with his finger. He takes a feather from a bird of prey, a buzzard or an eagle or not either, death and freedom seeming one to me tonight, I cannot tell. He stuffs the feather into a prayer stick and the prayer stick is on fire.

My desert mother sings lower. Her desert voice descends. Only the patient and I do not sing. Smoke out the smoke hole, tongue of the song, all voices out of one mouth, as the smoke rises. Song so deep in the throat the lips don't move. Sound is everywhere. Short sequences of song fall away at the end, like tape failing, time failing, ending in the silent present, return here.

God exits.

Dear god, you taught me this:

We pray, we sing, we pause to breathe. We call it living when in fact it's waiting for the return of something living, and when something living does not return, we may split in many parts and go off walking over territories no one sees but the schizophrenic; we may thirst and thrive on the single mind's oasis; we may go blind to darken the desert night, be no longer drawn to flickering stars, or hook our eyes on the crescent, dangle there; we may fall down and hear untethered music driving against headlights down asphalt in the rain, inducing god's seizure and biting off our tongue; or we may go on singing until the words themselves become the living end.

Once, I heard my name said with kindness.

bozo

My suburban mother slings words across a formica table. The light hangs from the ceiling; too low, it cuts off her forehead. Bastard! she screams. Motherfucker, I answer. I slam my hand into the lamp and the light above us goes out. Dawn. Bozo Circus intro music, the colour set, boys and girls, it is six a.m. The inflatable dinosaur drifts across the pool pissing air through a slow leak. Dawn, and my parents are entombed in the livingroom, while the ring leader, Mr. Ned, drenched in a bucket of water, cries loudly Boooozoooooo, and the clown waves his white gloved hands to the descending notes of the disappointed saxophone, pan of the bubble-gum audience, Colgate smile. I am home. My parents were waiting for the police to phone back when I walked in the front door. Now the lamp above us swings, blacks, and the sun rises. The sun rises but my mind is not here. Dawn enters with bent head.

My father says quietly, You scared the living-day-lights out of us. What are you thinking of? My mother screams, What do you think of that?! Nothing.

I am thinking of darkness outside. Somewhere outside this controlled world is dawn, and in the desert, the god-man is dropping his mask, looking for water to get the clay off his belly, and to feel the early morning come to life on his skin. Rub his dancing feet. I want to kiss his skin. God's mask lies on the floor, a pinch of corn pollen placed on the mouth. How does it taste? I want to lick the bird off of his forehead. This is what I am thinking. Should I tell them? It is the first sexual feeling of my life.

Father pulls his face down with his hand. He is gaunt, lips like a scythe. Father scrapes a chair along the floor and gestures me to sit. Synthetic sparks in the dry air. He does not cry. I am looking for one tear only, to catch in a small glass vial and hold to the light. But he does not cry. Mother slavers in the doorway, Little ungrateful bitch! But there is music in my mind. Father says red-faced, You must never do this again.

To be done it must be done again. In the hogan, a sequence is enacted like a hypothesis proven, and it must be repeated perfectly. I should tell my father this. He is a political scientist at a university. He would understand repetition, if only as the curse of nations, faces exchangeable, events reconstituted, infinite players of one plot, war up war down. As if the pattern were necessary, as if someone with great authority said, replicate. In the desert, there is an unknown order to me that frightens me. Everything laid out on the mask of God. Just so. Like eruption placed the ash and mountains, maybe just so. Just so and I thought it random.

Is the universe an accident? I ask.

What do you say, you are so ugly?! screams my mother. She rips at her skin, tears at her bathrobe. I have read that this is a Hebrew gesture of disinheritance. You are not my son, anymore, Jeremiah announced, ripping at his clothes.

a navajo story

It was Scavenger's First Day in the sky. When the eagles, who loved him, flew off to hunt, they said, Do not leave the house, for it is dangerous in the sky. If Scavenger had obeyed, there would be no story, there would be empty contentment. But Scavenger did leave home. He went looking for water. And Buzzard shot him down with a bean, and killed him, just like that, because Buzzard hates everyone. Buzzard is the bean-shooter, chief of the witches, and the story would end there if Buzzard weren't bitter and greedy and ugly as infertility, loving games like torture. One game he played was called Resurrection, which is easy for a witch.

The game begins like this: Scavenger is dead. The eagles are distraught. Buzzard says, enjoying this gap, We gonna play a guessin game, ladies an gentlemen. What ya gonna give me, feathaface? You gotta make me an offerin. But you gotta guess the RIGHT offerin. I not even gonna give you a clue. Get it right, or ya baby gonna be dead fera loooong time.

The eagles cheated. Big Fly landed on Buzzard's brain. Big Fly, being tiny and low in the food chain, was excellent at espionage. He tended to go unnoticed. So when Big Fly heard Buzzard's brain click, he whispered the small but necessary information into the eagles' ears. This way the eagles guessed the offering: a fatty piece of venison and a roll of tobacco. And Buzzard, outraged but bound to the rules of his own economy, placed the offering on his foot to show that he accepted. He spat, and Scavenger returned to life.

So it was the Second Day in the sky. The eagles went to hunt, and Scavenger stayed home. The eagles warned Scavenger not to touch any of the small, blue water jugs that hung beside the windows. Scavenger thought he would touch just one of the small, blue water jugs. He took just one of these small blue jugs down from its place in the window. He held the small blue jug between his large brown hands and looked at the water inside.

Unable to contain the very clouds themselves, he lost his balance and rain flooded the earth. Plants, insects, humans, jackrabbits, pinion mice and prairie dogs were drowning. And in the sky, Scavenger was humiliated. He ran away from home.

He ran straight into Spider's web. Spider wanted to suck his blood. She skipped like raindrops over her weaving. She lay beside him naked, beautiful, sexy and deadly. Scavenger almost wanted her. Wanting her, his tongue swelled up. She said, Aren't you powerful, drowning all those innocents on earth?! He blushed. Spider reached blackly for his neck, and his legs swayed open for her teeth. But just as she touched him, Black God, god of fire and a furious lover, breathed. Spider belonged to him. She leapt away blazing.

It was the Third Day. While the eagles hunted, Scavenger, more accustomed to his world and its dangers, went walking. The One-who-goes-about-picking-up-discarded-things went walking, and walked into a witch who had taken on the body of a coyote. Because the witch wanted sex with the Scavenger, she changed him into a coyote. Now they were the same species and compatible. But Scavenger was disgusted, and ran away in his coyote body.

He ran until he was lost. He had forgotten the simple rules: to pray for safety always one step before you, and never to trespass beyond the four mountains. Between the four mountains, the gods are surely yours, they stand within and hear your prayer and your prayer is your armour. Do not go beyond your prayer, or you may die. Scavenger had forgotten. He wandered into a far away country. He fed on rotting carrion. And he howled to no one's heart.

The eagles flew over the canyons looking for their son. Or was she a daughter? They could not find him. They found nothing except a coyote in midday howling. But because the coyote howled at noon, and bowed his head and swayed it, and tore at his skin with his fangs, and scratched at his muzzle as if he were tortured with thorns, the eagles became suspicious.

The eagles made a hoop. They swooped upon the coyote, and forced him through the hoop, and the coyote skin cracked around the head. They forced him through another hoop, the coyote skin peeled along the shoulders. They forced him through a third hoop, his torso hung around his hips. A fourth time they forced him, and the bloody flesh-bag of a coyote sank to Scavenger's feet. Now Scavenger was free of his false body.

It was the Fourth Day in the sky and the worst. Scavenger went walking. Black-tailed swallows dove at his head, danced on the cliffside, created a landslide, and buried Scavenger alive beneath a small mountain of rocks. The eagles, alerted by the landslide, came flying. They flew so fast that they broke the wind up beneath their wings, and small winds fell to the ground and swept away tumbleweed. When they reached him, Scavenger was buried.

The eagles were too small to shift the debris and uncover their loved one's body. So they called upon the hunters, wolf, lynx, bobcat and badger. Wolf, lynx and bobcat wore down their claws digging for Scavenger's corpse. They groaned as the rocks tore their fur from their skin and their skin from their bone, and still they'd uncovered nothing. Only badger, who was accustomed to self-immolation in the pursuit of food, dug right down under the earth and returned to the surface, bearing Scavenger's bones.

Clearly, much time had passed. Scavenger had decomposed, even in this climate where life breaks down so slowly and remains to haunt you. Now the mountains are weak with Scavenger's blood. They are trembling. The corn is ill with fever, cold and worms. The sound of Scavenger's death has entered the earth and run with the river, become the thunder of falls. And the flapping of eagle wings.

His bones in a heap at the bottom of a cliff, like this one. The eagles looking at each other sadly. Now, only witchcraft is possible. Now, good and evil are at a stand-off, and both must bow to necessity and love. Although witchcraft has been performed several times already in this story, it has been performed only by witches. Amongst the Navajo, witches are hideous things. But the eagles loved Scavenger so much that they called upon necessity and therefore *hóchxó*, which means the ugly, the unhappy, and the evil. The Navajo say that *hozho* (good) and *hóchxó* (evil) are inseparable conditions, suitable for humankind. *Hochxo* is abhorred, but it is welcomed to gain the power to drive it away. The degree of danger and power are equivalent. And to perform witchcraft, or resurrection, you must call on very unusual and very powerful forces.

Because they loved their child, the eagles performed witchcraft. The eagles lay Scavenger's bones on unwounded buckskin. They sang. And their song brought their voices and their visions down to the filthy bottom of the world, as nightmares do. From the song and the nightmare, if you are unlucky or weak, you will not return, you will die. But if you are lucky (or should I say blessed? or should I say holy?) the laws of the universe will fold under your wings, become air, bend, become wind, in its last definition, become nothing; the laws will become simply useful for your flight.

This way, the eagles brought their child back to life. And when their child had learned to die and resurrect, he flew. And when he flew, he flew higher and wove rainbows.

apostrophe

She says, See the worlds? There been lotsa worlds. The Holy People keep comin up from one world to the next through the hole. An now all them worlds are under us. In the canyon.

Can I fly above them? I ask.

You crazy?

No.

You holy?

No.

You dead?

No.

Eagle crying, she says. She points with her lips. Sometime Eagle take people through the hole in the sky. But the people gotta be holy or dead. Eagle took Scavenger.

Who?

Echo.

This world the fifth world. It last.

There are no more?

She walks on, saying nothing for a long while.

sand and the women

mother

she is dragging her stick in the snake-dust   a curved line is
        on her mind now   big skirts of sky and yellow
sheep   and the spaces between her teeth for sleeping stories

how long have I been here   who are you
back and forth in my mind changes
                        putting back clocks when cicadas scream coils
unleashed from the cuckoo   a trite european metaphor
for chaos   she says nothing   she is thinking about
time that is the same as this
                        simultaneity in the empty stretch
somewhere so much is happening

yet here is bare   sheep and miles sun on her head   dogs   jets
seed turning over wind   she is dragging her stick in
the snakedust   looking up from dust at me closed eyes
shield them   so she can see mine

What she looks like? I call her my desert mother. She looks like the desert.

the desert

She is like this: an unguessable age, a swollen warmth. Her face, not deep-ploughed, but in bloom, in age like a cactus in the night. Her hands bleed and scar. They are worn out and strong and as useful as legs. Hack off her breast if you have to lose something, but don't take her hands away. Their skin changing colour from wool dye. Hot spots on knuckles. Her palm is glazed by the rusted axe, seeping flax, smacking dough. She pours everything through her body, which is a by-pass, which is a vessel, which is a tool, not a machine, and does not lose itself in usefulness. Her millstone, curved out deeply. Every seed, grain, weed through her grip. The heal of her palm pounds yucca into soap or yucca into rope. Binding the horse, binding the sheep, a mother giving birth, crowning, ringing her black hair, wetly, over the fire, yucca suds squeezed out. She is like this: round as water, made of brittle grasses. She makes sounds. She screamed as she sent her husband away. He rushed at the hogan door with a big red fist, left a hole in the door where the sun comes through every dawn. Sun is a beautiful man. Sun knows no boundaries. She is like this: alone.

She wears homemade socks. She wears soil to her knees. She wears strands of sheep lint clung to her blouse. She wears an old beige jacket stained with earth and dung. Two wind-tattered scarves on her slipped back hair, loop in the chignon like tarmac in ice or orchids tied in a ribbon in spring. She wears her hair back off her brown neck, tied with a white rope. She wears turquoise to the sings. She wears a prairie-skirt and a velveteen blouse. Her velvet is almost a colour, purple and drinkable. She wears the days back to the turn of the century when the Navajo quit their buckskin breeches and woven dresses, and took up the look of teachers and missionaries and other foreign agents. She wears history.

history

1864, the military forced her grandmother to walk three hundred miles to a plot of land on the Pecos River. Those who dropped en route were shot, and hundreds of her kin were left unburied on the road side, their rigid bodies like stone markers pointing home. Two thousand Navajo walked, the long parade followed by coyotes.

The Americans had given a promise: the military would kill the Navajo if they did not walk and would feed them if they did. It was a promised prison, a small patch of green. No crops, houses, gardens, or fruit trees, but the land so impregnated with salt that the fields were as bare as the streets of Washington and their own starvation. The Gazette reported, As in the First Paradise so in this its Second Edition we pursue the even tenor of our way with nothing to mar the perfect harmony of the scene... the leopard lies down with lamb... the warlike savage has beaten his spear into a pruning hook...

Who knew that the water on that stretch of the Pecos River was poisonous? That the nearest mesquite roots for building strip-houses were eight to ten miles away? The nearest firewood twenty-five miles. Who can say exactly who was responsible in the trail of bureaucracy when the military halved the rations of beef and halved the rations of beef again and the Navajo searched among horse-dung for the grains voided whole? People competed with crows for food, and the crows triumphed. The soldiers offered hungry cocks to both men and women. That winter, due to insects, the crops failed, and her grandmother was just a girl who submitted to sex for a pint of corn.

She was not even a woman when she took the soldier's cock between her lips. But I didn't want to become a woman, I wanted to become a bird.

history

and there's a moaning and clucking the birds perching bug-eyed
banging their wings on the rocks making time pass

history is time changed and this was a day where there should be
no black and red

purple plum trees in the canyon
do not go beyond the mountains ever again

the fleshy pulp of her fingertips turning knobs picking plums
hot juice on my stuck lips

I think of eve my grandmother but my desert mother says bah
I tell you about first woman

First Woman

First Woman was the first holy one, along with First Man and Coyote. First Woman was real sexy and that was the beginning of many things. She started from nothing. First Woman was a bitch and that was also a beginning. Why wouldn't she be? First Woman would have been called a "tough dealer" if she was a man, and the world would have begun with less resistance and more identifiable heroics. First Woman was alone. First Woman was an egotist. First Woman was in love with love and herself. First Woman was holy. She had a hard-on. She had a husband. She modelled herself on nothing present. First Woman was an entrepreneurial saint. She investigated. No one investigated her so she did it herself. What have we here? She smelled her crotch. She smelled bouillon cubes and roses in her crotch, but nothing came to mind because nothing existed. It was the beginning and there were no metaphors.

First Woman was a wet scrap rung out after cleaning. First Woman complained all the time and bent the world this way and that, like nose cartilage after a fist fight. First Woman said dark wind, blue wind, yellow wind, white wind, which was the wrong order of invocation of wind and she knew it. She was bad. She was beautiful. This way First Woman changed prayer into witchcraft because she wanted it that way.

First Woman made ghost sickness, because she had a foul temper. First Girl and First Boy had made her angry. They put the wrong shoe on her wrong foot. First Woman was wilful. First Woman was unhappy, smashing her fists against empty space, the stones in her bracelets shattering like flint on empty space, made fire. So she made genitals from jewels. She was inspired. Coyote tugged his goatee and garnished the genitals with tufts. Now Holy People knew desire and pleasure and hunger and saturation. First Woman accomplished much by whatever means.

First Woman's mother was the daybreak, her father was the-yellow-light-after-the-sun-has-set. First Man's mother was the night, his father was the-blue-above-the-place-where-the-sun-has-set.

the story of the separation of the sexes

First Man came home. First Man was also good and bad. First Man had a pouch of evil. First Man had lust and temper, but today he was looking good. In wire shoes, blue woollen stockings, skin breeches down to the knees, fastened by silver buttons, white hunting shirt and scarlet cap, blanket thrown over his left shoulder, being right-handed on the horse, First Man came home looking just fine. He found his house dirty. His children starving. His wife out. Shit.

First Woman had gone out to play with her lover. In her black robe with its red border, she'd rolled in the horse dung piles. She rolled with her lover inside her, so as not to spread his scent all over her skin. His smell was sweet, like dark caves, but she shouldn't bring it home.

First Woman came home filthy. She stood in the middle of the hogan, a dwelling made octagonally of earth. Nodded at her husband. She weighed the air by its heaviness on her chin. Mutton, she said, softly, being a woman. She knew her job, got cooking. Then paused. She ran her greasy fingers through her apron, squeezed her crotch.

What the fuck? asked First Man.

Just giving some attention to what all men wanna die for.

And First Man had nothing to say to that, so he stepped across the cooking fire. His gesture is lost to my history. I do not know what his action meant. Violation or trespass or absence? I do not know. My culture leaves me only wishes toward meaning. I can watch clothes turn in a tumble dryer. I can heat my anger on electric rings, and watch my mother make dinner. There is nowhere warm I cannot be touched. All other sides are walled. Hence, I cannot understand First Man's action. He sat across the cooking fire, untouchable.

After four days, First Man packed his skin bags. And with lances, bows and arrows, he went to find the useful and sacred hermaphrodite who lived in a male and female hogan simultaneously. He/she had not only breasts and penis and vagina, he/she also had cooking pots, baking stones, mill stones, brooms, spoons and dishes, louse killers, corn, seeds of gourds and squash and melons, milkweed, sage, tobacco and whatever only women keep including sex.

First Man tried the size of his/her vagina by measuring it with a Spanish penny. He also measured his/her asshole. It was even smaller. Yum. Satisfied, First Man thought, men can live without women. He gathered his men and they rode across the river, through the yellow bank of foam.

First Woman was happy to be rid of her husband but unhappy to lose her lover who, being a man, was obliged to leave. And yet, as proved by United States military survival tests in the desert, much time passes before women suffer. Women are resilient, having sources of fat as well as knowledge.

The men on the other bank of the river had it all. They had the hermaphrodite and his/her gear, no power of creation and nothing to fear. The women on the original bank of the river had no hunting equipment, and without lances or bows and arrows, the female diet was limited. Without men, the women's vaginas had dreams that walked away at night and the dream of the woman and the dream of the vagina often travelled in separate directions, creating unbearable tension. So First Woman searched out several natural objects. As medicine for the sexual drought, she whittled and polished an assortment of dildos. Because women have the power of creation, these dildos satisfied and dangerously impregnated.

A woman made love to a young elk horn, still fuzzy with growth, and conceived a horned-monster. A woman made love to a feather quill and conceived a monster-eagle. A woman made love to a leg sinew and conceived a tracking-bear. A woman made love to a sour cactus, carved to a fine point, and conceived monsters-that-kill-by-eyes.

Naayee, the Navajo word for monster, means, abstractly, what-gets-in-the-way-of-life. These conceptions arose in the time of the Separation of the Sexes when there was no love. In storytelling this is the distant past, but the Navajo language employs the repetitive tense. Monsters are conceived. Monsters are conceived again. (First the Spanish came, then the Americans. The conquistadors, then the army, then the settlers, then the suburbanites. Me.)

history

1539. *Naayee* first arrived in the form of Coronado with one thousand horses, silver armour and silver cutlery, riding north from Mexico City in the pursuit of the Seven Golden Cities of Cibola. They found, instead, a series of small mud villages and, after much killing, returned home. 1595. *Naayee* arrived a second time in the body of Onate with four hundred colonists and seven thousand sheep, cows, mules, hogs, horses and jack-asses. The colonists introduced wool. They also introduced scalping. Gold was exchanged between the Santa Fe govern-ment and the thirsty settlers for every decibushel of dripping head flesh. Native souls were saved by baptism before their hosts were duly beheaded. The Pueblo people were burnt alive in their earth homes. Mountains became weak with human blood, the colour of human blood indecipherable to the white men; and the subsidiary races enslaved. Warriors were shot and women were raped, then sold, crouching in their discharge, for the price of a rifle and a mare and a shirt and thirty-five packs of gun powder. Children were sold for four knives, two fanegas of corn, four blankets, six yards of cloth and one plug of tobacco. Half the Navajo population disappeared into prairie skirts and chains. Baptised, they remained unreturnable by treaty. Baptised and blood-soaked before they were washed, they were wards of the Faith before they were beaten. Some were made charwomen. Some were made cooks. Some, whores. Some murdered in the night and fled. Adobe houses were painted white after every bat-tle. Twenty treaties were signed in disappearing ink and ground water. Riding over rivers of their own blood, the Navajo became masters of the horse and could not stop to drink. Living only on adrenaline, the Lords of the Earth, as the Spanish called them, appeared unconquerable, merely depletable as Spain remained financially disinterested in the northern territories. Convicts were sent by Mexico City to inhabit the uninhabitable north. Querechos, meaning enemy, meaning Navajo or Apache, were accused of every crime. Every citizen was armed and obliged to kill. Every Querecho death was a justice done to the future that was coming before Christ. Missionaries ate Jesus to protect them from witchcraft. Wine froze at midnight in the chalice, winter.

changing woman

who was born to give birth, and rid the world of monsters

First Man found a baby on Gobernador Notch, where dark clouds hung and dark birds sang and slight rain fell only. Was she born and abandoned or not born, just being? First Woman lay the baby on a cradle-board wrapped in splinters of rainbow. First Woman named the baby, A-woman-she-become-time-and-again. So Changing Woman got her name. She would grow young in spring, old in winter, bending like a woman's back. Arching sex was spring. Carrying a heap of logs was winter.

Changing Woman would bend like a beam of light, but she would bend herself, no one to bend her. It was the beginning. Some say it took four days, some say four years, to raise her. But when Changing Woman had risen, it was she who made us, Earth Surface People, though there was no pressing reason to make us. Just that, she was lonely, in the holy emptiness.

as when I emerge from my bath

It was like this: after a blue-hot day, Changing Woman made us from her skin beneath her breasts. She's so wet. She just scrapes us off her skin with her fingernail. She just blows on the grey sweat clay under her fingernail. Pinch of cornmeal. Says a prayer. And there we are, people.

In one version, Changing Woman's skin became shell which in turn became human. This explains how some of us continue without innards.

sounds of bodies

the beginning of the world

nebular hypothesis

A large globular mass of hot gas slowly went round in circles. As the gas cooled the glob became smaller and therefore went round quicker. Going too fast, the glob became flattened, and the earth and all other planets were thrown off as if from a merry-go-round. Weeee. Let me be a child again. Finally, the flat glob condensed to become the sun.

another hypothesis

The sun was originally part of a binary star, one half of a two-star system which revolved about a common centre of gravity. The other star exploded, and many planets, including earth, formed from its debris. We are an exploded sibling star longing for our twin. Whichever way you look at it, there is hunger, garbage, and alienation.

one of many catastrophe theories

All catastrophe theories treat the planets as interstellar accidents. They are faithless. One theory has it that the sun travelled alone in space until it was disrupted by a road accident with another star. Fortunately for everyone, it was only a near collision, but the tidal forces, generated by mutual gravitational attraction, drew out a stream of hot stuff from the surface of the sun and this hot stuff was pulled along by the passing star like a loose fender. This seems unreasonable as the sun was the larger object, but, anyhow, globules formed and became planets.

doubt and the modern age

Scientists admit that they are confused. No one is sure of themselves as they were in the Renaissance and the Age of Enlightenment. But it is generally believed that the beginning contained a proto-sun, a gas-glob and cosmic-glue, possibly including the action of ice and/or electrostatic or magnetic forces.

a brief contemplation on time

At the time of the beginning of the planets, a day lasted roughly an hour. The Earth has been slowed steadily, by the pull of the moon these forty-six thousand million years. The moon, that men are in love with, dangling rockets from her earlobes, is dragging lethargy through our bone marrow. Eventually, we will be slowed to such an extent that one day will be a lunar month, the same as my own body, whose sluggish light is only a reflection.

history

No world except this one was suitable for humans, and this world, the Navajo say, is the end. The last in a long succession. Floods, droughts, wars, and starvation forced our predecessors to climb through the worlds always in search of new worlds. No world was large enough for their desire. And though the space between the worlds is infinite with stars, each new world appeared so small and twirled around so quickly that everyone was giddy. Thoughts flew out of them in shards, made wars, and they climbed up again, hoping.

history

Most of the people she knew as a child are dead now. Henry was shot in the honky-tonk. Donny died in jail, internal bleeding. LaRosa got influenza, a disease like her pretty name. Meg's boy played with Meg's gun and blew a hole through Meg's baby. The baby's alive, but he can't talk. Don't talk about Meg's boy. The boy hung himself two days later. No one knows what killed old Erma, maybe greed, maybe hunger, maybe phlegm in the lungs, she was a bitch, probably a witch. Nah, she says, too stupid. Gallstones. Ghost sickness. Ghosts hate the livin. They jealous, she says. Like the livin are jealous of the even-more-livin. Got too much light in you eye, you neighbour gonna spit in you eye to dark it. That the way the world is now. It goin dark now like the beginnin. Junior knifed Mary.

the dead

She lays down her knife, clutches the dead goat with her fist and rips the skin off gently, releasing a sound like peeling glue, or peeling jeans from my wet legs, or cellophane from dinner in the microwave, suburbs. I remember my mother's lips were white with booze. The goat skin clings to the muscular sinew. And my father was a martyr, the sacrificial body. What has become of these people? How long have I been here? The goat-mama's screaming in the background. Her baby died last night, got caught in the slats of the corral and couldn't breathe.

We're sitting in dry mud. Rotten sheep teeth smiling, they just keep smiling, chewing, the stench of them bulging like sex. My desert mother saws the last flesh from the carcass. Cl'isi, she says, baby goat. And I catch the blood in a tin can for cooking, lay the muscular skeleton on the dirt. Without its skin, the body looks tender and foetal. Tendrillar. I push its limby death to the side. Something will want to eat this baby, baby-o. Leave it to the birds.

The goat-mother mourns, milk draining out of balloons. We want to replace the dead with the living, hoping the mother will take to her teat an orphan whose goat-mama died giving birth. It would seem that nature has a way of fitting together, but it doesn't. The mother won't feed unless the scent is right. Like a renaissance masquerade, like someone in the wife's bed on a black night full of balconies, like a ritual of hoops, the orphan will wear the skin of the dead cl'isi.

I throw the skin-cape over its torso. The cape is white with small blood roses and I remember my christening gown. I shove the head into the skin-hood and remember the tassels on my plastic yellow raincoat when I was three years old. I think, I want a baby too. Like dressing up a Chihuahua. The queen of Heart's pig in bonnet. Got four ears.

                                                                masquerade

My mother told me this: Scavenger lived many years in the sky with eagles. When the eagles came home at night, they took off their feather clothes, which opened down the front. Inside were human forms in white suits, which were never removed.

transformation
and the significance of jumping through hoops

Hoops: enclosed space is under control, evil ousted and power harnessed. The patient absorbs the harnessed power by making a labyrinthic journey: a path of hoops. One night I witnessed the ritual of hoops in the exorcisitic cycle of the Big Star Chant. The patient was a woman, and over her head she wore a beautiful veil of simple unbleached muslin. Beneath the veil she was naked. It was time for bending beneath something that sounds beautiful.

In her arms she carried her few beloved possessions. Fewer than her beloved thoughts. She carried a dress, a necklace, a hair grip, a baby. She held what was important to her and could be held. She passed through the hoops the medicine man had made for her to pass through, hoops tied with dodgeweed, grama grass, rock sage, spruce. Hoops by which the medicine man would uncover her as if he loved her. As she passed through the black hoop, he slipped the unbleached muslin off her head. Through the blue hoop, her neck, yellow hoop, her shoulders, white hoop, her brown waist. Now she walked naked through hoops and what was it fell from her body? The next day the hoops were hard oak, black with soot of ground coal like sundown.

Sunset

The sun came through the hole in the door. The orphan goat, like a bloody dream, slept by our bed in a cardboard box. Our masquerade didn't work. It works or it doesn't, my mother says. The ewe butted the hell out of the impostor with her horns and we pulled it away to save its life. Small nickel-sized wound in the cl'isi's torso. We made a tourniquet of rags around its chest to stop the bleeding. Tomorrow, perhaps, we will kill it with a rock.

Now I fill a plastic bottle with Carnation concentrated milk and attach a plastic nipple. I watch the goat suck to the end of the world, bury my face in its new fur. I can touch it now, because no mother is ever going to touch it. I can rub my smell all over it. I can touch it because it is unwanted.

Sunset.

My desert mother and I drip cornmeal between our fingers like dry rain. Corn is *diyinni*, one of many *diyinni*, she says, holy people, gods. We don't give thanks like a Christian gives thanks, like *diyinni* don't need to help us. *Diyinni* need to help us. We make offerin to Corn so Corn can eat. The people feed the gods an the gods grow an the people grow. Both feed each other. By offerin the world is balanced. We don't need Christian humility, we jus need balance. Then the sun *diyinni* an the water *diyinni* an the corn an the moon an the earth an the stars an the birds *diyinni* get strong. Navajo people need the gods an the gods need Navajo people.

night

all black with soot of ground coal

At night it is always cold. Moon is *diyinni*, she says. Fire in the hogan. Fire is *diyinni*, she says. By the shadows we undress.

Something moans. Candied smell of kerosene exstinguished. I can make out nothing human or animal or insectoid, only the outer dark. The blanket swept from the door, smoke turns in the stove and rushes out the new exit. From the oil-drum fire, shadows through the hogan like the dark side of snakes. Tongues. Chimney whines. The wind's a riot. It sung the sun down, beat the sun down, rattles up the moon into the sky. I watch the stars through the smoke hole, to fall asleep by. Remember the sunset was a painted glory, folds of oil purple. Now stars, stars everywhere. The sky don't know how to be humble.

And the Night says, Who says so? I answer, don't know. And the Night says, Who are you? I answer, don't know.

and during the intervals between songs they shouted be be be be yo

things I am afraid of:

1. Identity.
2. Ending sentences with a preposition. (Where do you come from?
Where I come from you don't end sentences with a preposition, said
the bitch at my parents' cocktail party. Okay, I answer, where do you
come from, bitch?)
3. I go home, I come back. (I am a schoolgirl remember?) I wash vigor-
ously when I'm home and I am haunted. There is tv inside me anywhere I go. In the desert, stretch the silence and I still hear childhood
voices devouring the spaciousness. Even when I come back, even when
I go home. Sheep are so small in this landscape. Sheep never let me
touch them. Sheepish like the meaning of a sentence said after years of
bitter history. Let me say, what I cannot touch unnerves me.
4. I am afraid I do not like to say my name anymore. I am afraid of
everything that continues to create me undefined: God, Parental
Guidance, Standard of Living, Homeland. Such exist only by virtue of
the words themselves. I am choked with words. I cannot put the script
down in my head. In the day I am walking with mute sheep, hot as
God's mouth, from which everything that falls is a word. It is thorn. It
is sheaf. It is the juice of soapweed. God is holding pinion nuts in one
side of his mouth, passing them one by one through his back teeth,
cracking each as it passes, and letting the shells fall from the other side
of his mouth. I am hot. The word is dust. I am hot. The word is dirt. I
am hot. Talus and scree, mass rock debris that weathered down the
mountain, rockwaste, sliderock. The word is fragment. It is a residue
that completely mantles the origin, like memory. I don't know that
these fragments are entirely correct. I am alone, it is winter, it is cold,
there is nothing called Christmas, Icarus, Charon. All those mythic
names to beat my head against. I am on the cliff top, collecting wood
before sundown, to put the fire dancing before the stars, before the heat
slips off the earth, cloudlessly. But thought does not slip off of me.

Cornelian girl out in the male rain, you have no god to call upon, but you and the bluebird and all kinds of grasshoppers are close.

night

Curl close I hear her sleep, she will rise at dawn, pray with yellow cornmeal, powder her hands in white flour and shuffle fry bread between her palms, throw it on the flame and eat her fingerprints. She will open the corral, count one hundred and nineteen sheep and twelve goats who have no names and yet she knows each one. She walks three miles to a water hole, six more miles for the sweeter grasses, then milk the goats and taste the sweeter grasses in their milk. She will pen the sheep like parking the truck, pause for the sundown, pray with white cornmeal, throw mutton scraps to the dogs who maim each other fighting, throw dishwater at the dogs to stop their fighting, and sweep the hogan dirt about, pound it with the broom, see the moon up through the bristles, bow her head over mutton stew and fry bread and peanuts and coffee, and then she will sit at the loom and weave the cliffs, the pass of ghosts who cannot love each other because ghosts cannot love each other, the place of bitten tongues, discarded things. She will take down her hair, and her white ribbon flies. Scavenger went up on the wings of snakes, she says. She will blow out her candle and sleep heavy.

But night is no longer a perfect silence, a perfect o, a fingerprint closing. Loud night. Pick-up engines gunning, someone running drunk. Coyotes, owls. I wake and fall asleep again and wake again. Stars move beyond my grasp. I must go home tomorrow o o o. Sharp wing over the smoke-hole makes a shadow on the floor. Ashes in the sunfire drowning in the swimming pool.

twins:

one-who-arranges-scalps one-who-slays-monsters-here-and-there

mother

I walk through the name-plate door, orange-hue of the self-conscious livingroom. My desert mother has dropped me at the corner of the block, says nothing as I jump from the pick-up. She is now in the sound of the engine turning over, stopping for the red light, as the rain runs down the line of my long neck. She should have driven straight through the red.

It is raining. It is hot. Is it always hot or is it always cold?

Mommy wears a red dress with flowers. My fingers shake the water from my ears. Tuck my lips inside my teeth, slip my coat on a hook, my brown teeth. Ice cubes rock in the the Arctic, the public broadcast nature special, this world, this tv. Mommy?
    You're home.
    I'm late.
    It's you.
    Yes.
    Mommy reeks of gin. Reeks is the only good word for drunk stench. My father raises his head from his paper. Simultaneous opera. I see the rhythm in his eyes. My father smiles and disappears deeply in his armchair. With the corner of the newspaper, he folds a mottled crane. Finally my mother screams. She screams at my father about the shit on my boots and bad influences. I imagine Christ's wounds were made by her stilettos. And my father, quietly, doesn't defend me. Unfolding the paper bird into an advertisement for shoes. You'd better change, he says, we're going to have a Christmas party.   Faintly, I answer him, humming:

excerpt of song from the enemy way
translated by Jesuit Father Berard Haile

the enemy woman was brought here
she is brought inside
eyea ena xalayai
when her dream did not come true
and she had to die
emergence women began rejoicing
they began flute playing
e ya eina xalayai ene ya
now warrior so and so by name
kills them for me
his enemies he usually slays for me
if you continue so for me
i shall despise my husband for your sake
i get restless to prostitute myself
as my skirt sounds its swish swish
i swing my foot back and forth
yah rah ai his tail tail tail
yah rah ai his tail
as my skirt sounds its swish swish
i tiptoe along i tiptoe along
rah yah ai his tail tail tail

the party

Meatballs? asks Mommy, holding out a tray. A fly sucks juice out of a meatball. The monsoon kills the worms in the garden, but there aren't many worms in a desert garden, one reason for the stiffness of the earth. I watch rain fall on a cactus blossom, closing. Black umbrellas hang like drenched bats in closets, the wind is high, and the front door opens and shuts. The guests are coming in.

See that woman's fingernails? a man asks another man, plying a toothpick in his teeth. I hate those long red fingernails. Why do women do it? It must come from the Chinese.

The men gesture at a fat woman by the sideboard with red nails. She flounders, undecided: will she have a chocolate nob? A blue earring on her bilious face trembles.

Yes, please do, says my mother.

The fat woman wavers slowly, appraises her reflection in the enormous gilt mirror behind the splay of snacks. How warm, how wet, how round, how red her mouth, how the luxuriant skin about her neck folds around her rhinestone crucifix like egg whites in meringue. And now she tries a chocolate nob, doesn't like the chocolate nob. It is neither hot nor cold, she thinks, it is neither good nor bad, lukewarm, she spits the chocolate nob into a napkin, deposits it somewhere with painted fingers.

It's a fetish, says the man. I'm sure it comes from the Chinese.

Outside in a tree, a crow calls.

Cut his crowing head off. Hang him on a coat hook like a hat.

The Chinese are odd, the man continues. They take their canaries out for walks. Thousands of little yellow men, dressed in those stiff blue uniforms, walking yellow canaries in the dawn. They believe if the sun can't hear the canaries sing, the sun will refuse to rise. He laughs.

Salmon cracker, Fritzy? asks Mommy. The laughing man, still laughing, takes a salmon cracker from my mother and my mother, still offering, disappears. The man slowly cracks an incidental knuckle. Chews.

The female salmon, he says, or is it carp? — lays a million

eggs, one third her body weight, after the male has screwed her in the mud.

excerpt of song from the enemy way
translated 1908, censored by the Anthropological Society until 1938

now the ugly head bag of the enemy
of the enemy woman
lies scattered about
her baskets scattered
her ordure scattered
bones are scattered about
her corpse lies there rah rah
his tail tail tail
even before the sun stands high
big buzzard grips his penis
drags him along
and drags the corpse
to a suitable place rah rah
even before the darkness sets in
slim coyote grips her big toe
drags her along
and drags the corpse
to a suitable place rah rah
there is a strip of land
wood is scattered on this land
due to tears food is tasteless on this land
how sad sad they are lined up
they are lined up yah rah
the wind whistles the wind whistles
rah yah his tail tail tail

the party

Little flames passing lusts, guests' cigarettes reflected and count-
able in windows, I lean my head against the glass wishing my
hair would burn. Feel the stretch in my breaking neck. Breathe.
I breathe. I breathe until I am done breathing. I wrap my palm
around my lemonade, feel the cold as the glass sweats. Glass
edge. A red tight bloom bends my way in the garden and I drip.
Wine stems chime. Time and lusts are passing. There are new
thoughts in my mind. There is now more cognizant time
between creation and causality in my mind, now more hairy
wandering ancestry in my mind, more equality of sexual trivia
between the genitals in my mind, more happening in many
cities to divers body parts in my mind, more excuses in my mind,
more idle lounging in my mind, fondling in my mind, more
drunken observance of Christmas in my mind, more people,
fewer names, more corpses, and artefacts and stories found at six
foot stratum in continental digs between my legs, in my mind.
History is in continual proliferation. What museums cannot
house, toilet paper cannot absorb. And the present, incapable of
being defined even as a Polaroid, is hopelessly outweighted by
the collection of time passing, infested with the larvae of collec-
tions of all versions breeding. For the moment that time passing
is begun, it cannot stop except arbitrarily. The more you know
the more or less you are.

I am trying to remember the name of a disease. It is a mental
illness impairing direction. The patient can only exit the way
she entered. I think it must be raining on the Cliffs of the Dead
and the eagles will fold their wings to cover their child's head.
The Christmas party continues in the background of my spirit
like a game show.

song about my name

My name is made of water. Moving loosely over space. My name
is a mask of blue haze. I am a mirage. Everything that is beautiful
inside me is borrowed and passing.

shitting during the Christmas party

Anus open, closed. I crawl to the toilet until the party is over. I lean my head between my thighs spread flatly on the can. Outside I hear my mother, drunk. Raise my eyes from my flesh. Toilet walls. Behold the poster of da Vinci's woman with an ermine on her shoulder. I always thought it was a mongoose but now I've looked it up. ermine: any of several weasels that assume white winter pelage usually with more or less black on the tail / a large European weasel / least weasel / New York weasel / a trimming of ermine / a rank as of a king or lord or office as of a judge of which the ceremonial or official robe is ornamented with ermine emblematic of authority / a heraldic fur consisting of black spots.

I imagine my shit is an ermine. I imagine my shit is a kinky man's gerbil, victim of gerbiling as reported in the newspaper: one man stuffing a gerbil up another man's asshole, unable to retrieve it, lights a match to see it clearly, creating a flaming gas-ball that shoots the gerbil out of the anus, blinding the match carrier, scorching the asshole and killing the gerbil. I don't know which is worse. The fire ran right up that guy's large intestines. The policeman felt sorry for the gerbil. Its name was Harry.

Behold the little mirror on the opposite wall. The ermine also looks at the mirror, but sees nothing with its black eyes. Only the mirror sees. This is my momentary absorption and diagnosis of the unreal. Outside the door, my mother paces. As she resents my absence, I shit harder. See my way into the ermine, who I thought until today was a mongoose, and my way into the mirror, and live there forever in silent reproduction of my image.

She's taking forever, screams my mother outside the door, drunk.

other drunks or
beer laundry blood and guts

Nightshift splatterings of Bud, dribbling backwash and cigarette ash in the sand, empty-hump Camel packs ground under the heel of a disappearing cowboy boot, scorpion under the cellophane sleeping pink like a genital, a pile of shit, a heap of vomit, glare.

It was morning, and we were cruising for empties, drove off the dirt tracks, followed dry arroyos, found the night-haunts of drunk Navajo reeling. Aluminium cans would pay to wash the laundry. Look for it, she said. Everything worth living for happened here during the night and sank into the dirt, and the guys with thick eyelids sleeping off the buzz couldn't remember getting home or with whom or what home is anyway. But, they were gone and they had left us their beer cans and empty liquor bottles called deadmen in suburban 1950's slang.

(Outside the bathroom door, mommy laughs. I hear her tilt the bottle on the sideboard, playing a little déclassé, swigging down the last slug, smiling, saying, "deadman," swaying on her heels. Pat her plastic hair in the gilt mirror. No perfect silence in the evening anymore. Even the pat pat pat will drive you crazy.)

But only the beer cans pay for the laundry. My desert mother and I knee-deep in the ditch, stooping for everything that glitters silver under the violent sun, a necessary economy. We drive off the res, stop at the recycling plant and use the earnings in the industrial washing machines at the border-town laundromat. We don't wash clothes, we wash sheep skins, the corresponding musculature just unhooked from the butchering tree, intestinal sack like a businessman's paunch newly stuffed with gut for dinner. Across the street from the laundromat is the Home of the Royal Antediluvian Order of Buffalo.

Inside the laundromat, someone was chewing tobacco and

spitting in a coffee cup. Joe said, soothes my brain, Flo. (Yellow dribbles down his rut face. He's a regular.) Cooools my brain.

Shut up Joe, yer just a slob, said Flo. Flo was ironing a t-shirt that read: Which is better a beer or a broad? A cigarette hanging flawless from her lips. She works here. No fan. Fluorescent lights. Flies. She'll wash a busy man's underwear for three dollars and won't ask questions about any irregularities. Now, she stood on one foot, high heel scratching her red ankle scab through a tan nylon, the grain of the nylon moving slowly up and down.

A snot-faced boy picked his nose and ate it; earlier I suspect he was rubbing it all over his face. His mother's yellow perm fell slightly as the seconds passed. Short and Curly Look Perm. She ran her finger over her teeth and turned the next page of People Magazine, covetous of California glamour. Said, Stop picking yer nose. You wanna slap?!

An ironed smell in the air mixed with tobacco smoke and gob. White powder on the counters like someone ought to sniff it. A sad man waiting for his own wife's do at Sally's Hair across the street, where every fifteen minutes another sad woman with poofed hair slumped pretty and feathered or pretty and curly out the door, back to her car, trailing aerosol. The sad man mesmerized by the roundabout-video-laundro movement with his-and-her pyjamas coming clean in the interim.

A punk dropped his head in his hands, his boots went heavy and he was bored shitless by the laundro-radio-sympathy-music, that seeped from the wrecked transitor at the end of the fucking ironing board. His hangover.

Shit.

Nice language.

Fuck you.

I was plying the sheepskins from the garbage bag, direct into the laundro-barrel and they were clinging to the plastic like cheeky baboons. Bits of ligament hung to the leather, blood in the hair.

Radio-station fuzz-sound, played too low like a mosquito song, playing one unremarkable country ditty over the next fifteen minutes. Some interviewee said, I love Elvis not like I love my husband but like I'd love a member of my family, a brother. Someone said, he comes in dreams. Now the radio advertised 7 UP, Bank America, Oscar Myer Weiners, itself, Tim's, the Pawn Shop, Stella's Steak House — eat cheap, let lovely ladies serve — itself, The Night of the Stars.

The screen door to the outside had a hole in it. No one came through. A fly hovered and retreated. Heat from the outside and heat from the inside melted each other. Smoke settled in my palms and in the *v* of a newspaper (caption: invest confidentially in foreign markets, the fantasy is possible. image: white man towering above a swarm of Japanese) coming to rest in the speak-clouds of the comics. Words stayed still.

Whenever we do this, the window clots with blood. I pressed my back to the glass, crossed my legs, read the funnies in the twenty-cent paper, blocked the view from the customers, poured in a half box of Puff to overpower the stench, fresh as an abortion. My desert mother left me, went down the road to buy hotdogs with food stamps when the machine busted in mid-cycle, water and blood and flesh flung hard against the window like a breech in the hull of a submarine, highlights from Das Boot and Captain Nemo, but nothing going round. I shouted across the room, Hey! This thing's broken! Flo by the ironing board let a necktie slip to the floor, and limped over. She fiddled with some buttons. She sagged. Then said, Shit, ther's gonna be a mess. She hit a switch, turned the latch, and opened the door. Blood water.

Suddenly, everyone was screaming.

Murderer!

Scalping!

Filthy Indians!

Fucking cool! cried the punk.

I pissed in my pants. I always piss in my pants when I'm frightened. I said, Sheep! No one listened. I said, It's just sheep, shit what's the big deal! It's sheep blood, shit, haven't you ever been to a butchering!

Butcher!

What have ye done to that Lamb of God, Satan!
Psychopath!
Weirdo!
This is a respectful laundromat!
Look at my nylons!
Capital Punishment. The radio station announced Arizona's latest zapping, someone dying and all I know about him is the Laundromat. I also know he was twenty-one years old. People Magazine movie stars got covered in blood-water. The spotted necktie got covered in blood water. The snot-faced boy shoved his face everywhere. My desert mother walked in with hot-dogs.

The crowd turned on her. The crowd was screaming. She walked through the blood water. It wet the dung on her shoes. She drew the sopping skins from the broken machine. She took me by the hand and we walked out.

after the party

Si-igh-lunt night ho-o-ly night aaaall is calm aaaall is brrrright errround yon vi-iiir-gin muth-er and child, mommy humming, third stanza, mommy screaming

subsistence living

Exist: L. existere: to step forth, emerge, come into being, to have actual or real being whether material or spiritual, have being in space and time. **Subsist:** LL susistere: to stay alive, to have existence as a concept rather than in fact.

On Route 101, she sells two sheep skins to one tourist for ten dollars a piece. Statistic: white skins sell better than brown 95 percent of the time. Synonym: skin is money. Antonym: wealth is a different story. It is the story of sheep, goats, sheepdogs, horses, pigs, corn, watermelon, beans, baskets, blankets, feathers, jewellery, and sometimes a well, but usually not much of any of these. And trees, I forgot trees. Trees are wealth, medicine, shields. Juniper burns in the oil-can stove, wet and fresh and lit by kerosene. Old Indian trick, she jeers. She cuts down a live one and next a young one and there's nothing else in the desert. The desert becomes a greater desert. The sound of chain saws, bringing down trees, till the monsoons take off the top soil, and instead of the cold at night it is hunger, the season disintegrating, year down upon year, until finally the year is dead.

shitting after the party

This suckling coffin of a book.

I will build a tower of scrap, scavenge what I can from fragments, take what is mine from the meaning of corpses, longing. I will make an offering, something beautiful of offal, by the pattern of my own hands. I will walk the cliffs of the dead. Look, it is night out my window, below me, shit, and everyone is screaming. But look, I can throw words into the sky and make stars.

bloodsong and jet

time

Month of slender wind, month of snow crust, month of the eaglets, month of lost antlers, month of delicate leaves, month of swelling seeds, month of bloom, month of mountain sheep fucking, month when the antelope drop their fawns in the tumbleweed, month fruits ripen. There are thirteen months. Each month has a soft feather and a heart. Month of large leaves, wind is your heart, rain is your soft feather. January, morning star and ice.

Nostalgic crying, because to look is beautiful, is the origin of Navajo song.

tuesday morning

I spy the derelict pick-up by the blanketed door. I spy it is purple, wheelless, engineless, strangled rust under the blue sky. I spy
the red blanket. I spy a yellow tin can. I spy a red rooster, no
chicken in the yard, horny fowl, crazed widower, useless except,
now and then, as a guard dog. I spy black lazy bitches, docile.
What good are they? The rooster is like her ex-husband, maybe
is her ex-husband, mean bastard chasing visitors like grasshoppers. I spy grasshoppers. Today, there's a baby visiting with its
mother. I spy its sagging disposable Pampers in the dirt that are
going to be thrown on the dung heap. The baby's bald. I spy the
rooster peck its little fontanel. You should hear the baby scream
and the rooster screams too, but who knows why the rooster is
screaming. Some kind of hell-cry, the origin of music.

All song-stories are about heroes and the journey to become holy.

holy / spiritually whole, sound, or perfect: of unimpaired innocence or proved
virtue: pure in heart: godly, pious — often used in mild oaths / not capable of
being approached with impunity: filled with mysterious, super-human, and
potentially fatal power: dangerously powerful if violated — some words are considered so holy they must never be sung.

the rooster and the jet

The rooster is piercing a little girl's shins. I think she is my mother's niece, but relationship is never obvious. Kin is close, extensive and complex, sister and cousin often one and the same. Grandmother the word of age, mother the word of respect, daughter the word of love. The rooster pecks, bloodletting. The girl runs crazy with a broom, slamming the rooster while sweeping the floor. The rooster rears, slips through the bristles, upsetting the water jugs, dropping feathers, small dimes of shit, insane, going madder than the child, screaming, balking. The child slips on feathers. The child hides behind the hogan door, holding her nose because the air stinks. Hot chili burns on the stove top. The smell is almost unbearable, but it'll drive the spiders out. The little girl cries, but not from sorrow, her eyes pouring chili-water into the desert. She looks up through the smoke hole, a flock of seven jets appear in a *v* formation, fly low, break the sound barrier. So loud that it is almost noiseless.

White out. Blot out. Red chili. Feathers.

Outside, my desert mother stops her shoveling. We've been digging a second outhouse. Her skirt billows. Wind blows from great engines, and exhaust is torn away from the earth in a blue and polluted dispersal, invisible. She covers her ears and sways. This world becomes a deafened scene. Bodies running around the yard and you cannot hear the whoop or the tread of their feet. The reservation is considered sparsely populated and therefore suitable for military exercises. Many of the animals are deaf.

the enemy

translated by Father Berard Haile

I am afraid green frog now said, he told. Not I, I am not afraid, I said. Crawl below me here, I said, then he told. Then, as often as they [the enemy] would take a forward step to strike, their blows would glance off my body, they were cutting off their own legs. They could not succeed with us, he told.

her voice under stalactites

The cicadas won the world, she told us. The cicadas were the first of the Holy People to come through the hole in the world but this world was so wet those days that the cicadas had a great blue problem. The world was covered in cold water an the cicadas didn't know how to swim. This was the last world. This was they world, was the world of lotsa colours, was the only world where the People could be born an survive. But the cicadas had a big blue problem. When they came up, the cicadas fought the grebes.

Who are the grebes? asks her nephew arched over a rock, peeing. Steam off his pee. Tinkle. Ssss. Hot rod penis.

They were swimmers I guess, she says but she does not know. When the cicadas came up they had to learn how to swim. They were stuck in it. When they won the world, they stuck in it too. The world was too small an people kill other people when the world too small. So Blue God, like a white man with a stick a dynamite, threw four stones an split the cliffs an the water rushed out into mud an rivers. Smooth wind an desert. The cicadas were released an spread. Their song, your ear under water.

bhizhoni	beautiful
eeyah	scarey

...yinshyeh	my name is...
howan gondesta	I'm going home

as if silence were location I could visit

return to silence and then recede from silence   renunciatory
stretches   lengths of imagination   desert straining into
song and dropping off again   the origin   I remember
silence

between jet blasts   from my cradle small apricot ears
tuned to the long wave beyond the suburb there was a silence
and I gurgled was a silence and I peed   silence and I learned
my first words   *this world*

song represents this world   pollen represents this world
precious stones represent this world   to the Navajo but to
me jets represent this world

I remember   silence that jet fighters broke on the
day of my christening at the speed of sound   are you deaf?
my mother screams   hear her low low low scream

festivity

witchcraft

or christmas

Only what is holy can be inverted to witchcraft, for there is no other power in this world. First be holy, then you can warp yourself to your own design, assuming that's what you want: a basic luciferian model of evil.

The holy is disappearing. The Navajo songs are disappearing. I've met ninety-year-old medicine men with no apprentices. And since each medicine man is expert in only one or two sings, the lesser known sings will often die with a man. The relationship with the gods goes untended and belief falters, especially in the young. What remains is fear. At the end of all worlds, ghosts and witches gain power.

Why does the disruption of the holy survive when the holy doesn't? It is the threat of the disruption that survives. Without knowledge of the holy there cannot be true witchcraft and, yet, accusation of witchcraft is epidemic. Like a stray dog will go anywhere. Even the half-wit up the mountain became a coyote and killed a cow one night, if you believe what you hear, but today I don't.

I believe it is like this: in a failing society (is this a failing society?) someone has to be responsible for the end. (scapegoat) In America we sue the shit out of each other. Power exists amongst us if only in the threat of a deceased but resurrectable idea (Navajo witches blow on the dead, make them breathe again). Power exists as an idea pitted against an outer idea of power. People hope: someone amongst us must have power, even if it is for evil, someone *amongst* us must be destroying us, because if they are not then we are entirely powerless.

Very likely we are powerless. Very likely, only the Pentagon has power, or only the idea of the pentagon has power or only the rich have power behind sharp gates, chrome doors, tinted limo windows, invisible, and so only the idea of the rich has power, but all this is so far away from the blood, it is unsatisfying. It is deadly. When power is that remote, there is no one to hear the victim scream.

witchcraft

I am picking over bones. Where fingernails were once important. And every Monday, Mommy had her hair done before she
stopped brushing it at all. Her wedding dress erect and empty in
the livingroom, greeting guests, she was beautiful, being normal,
before she went utterly mad. Swizzle-sticks, potato-salad-parties.
Three-minute quicks, mashed-potato-flakes. Idiot-child, she
called me that. Hot dogs. Bitch. Big culture happening the
opening of two department stores. Grand refrigerator/freezer in
the basement. Don't you look fat! Don't stand their gawking,
choose something! Shave, she said. Which part of my body?
Weeds in a median strip. Don't trespass on the private. Don't
write it. Don't vote or your marriage will die. Superior Tire
Sponsored Baseball. Retired Barbie she's in college. And I wish
my body, I wish my body, super car and station-wagon of the
cross. Everything I own, my husband, my house, my dog, my
maid, my lawn, patio, family seats in front of the tv, trash, toys,
classic clothes, toasters. Throwing the bullshit out of the top-
storey window, being the least told story, which is the way with
violent houses. Shit on the lawn that arrived in six-foot rolls,
hit the freeway dreamhouse. Mommy, you were anorexic at fifty,
drunken at sixty, Selah. Pilsbury Doughboy drowned in the
swimming pool. What do you want, a people's history of the
U.S.? Adventures in the unknown interiors?

christmas

Mother complains as she cooks in her heels about her varicose vein. The line in the tablecloth leads to my sister, skips up her buttons and slides round her catty blue eyeliner, (little lift at the corners) catapulting over her carefully parted hair and the line falls off her back. (I have an older sister who I have neglected to mention.) The four of us eat and talk about school. My sister has memorized all the acid compounds of the universe. Nitric, she says. Ascorbic, she says. No one says anything of the annual mass and how the communion wafer is presently being attacked by amino acids. My father says nothing at all. Mother says how much she paid for our presents.

Christmas night, my sister washes the silver that cannot go in the dishwasher and sorts the turkey bones that cannot go in the garbage disposal, cursing the limits of technology. She catches grease drippings in a coffee can. I fold wrapping paper for next year.

My mother comes down in her nightgown, opens the fridge. She is flooded with light like an icon. What does she look like? She has hung her image incrementally on walls. In the stairwell, on the seventh step, she wears her big-flowered linen wedding gown in glossy black and white and formulated breasts beneath. In the stairwell, on the eighth step, she wears her petite-black-wool number, from her wedding trousseau, fitted just-so snugly, as she sits on a snarling carousel horse, painted, smiling, her sheerest nylon legs, before the first birth and the red veins, on honeymoon in the capital city. In the stairwell, ninth step, she does not exist at all. The grandfather clock ticks cruelly on the landing. Rape what I rape, eat what I eat, says the hour.

Where is the ham? she asks.

What ham? asks my sister.

The ham. Where's the ham?

I had some earlier, says my sister.

There's no ham here! The ham is gone! Where's it got to?

I don't know.

There was some. When did you have the ham?

I don't know. I don't remember.

You can! If you wanted to you could! When are you eating ham?!

My sister looks at the clock. Looks at me. I drop my eyes and begin to fold an origami bird out of the wrappings.

I don't know. Yesterday. The day before. What does it matter? There's no ham! That's what matters!

There's no ham in this refrigerator. What are you doing?! You ate all the ham, and you don't know when? As if you're stealing down here in the night and eating ham! I come down on Christmas wanting ham and you cannot even tell me when you ate the ham, where it's gotten, why there isn't — where are you going?!

It's late. I'm tired. There's turkey in the side compartment.

That's wonderful. Just wonderful. You and your sister hide yourselves away on Christmas night. Leave your father sitting on his own on Christmas night. Joseph! My father has a name. She yells up the stairs, Joseph, come down here! He's your father, do you hear me? He's wasting away upstairs. I'm starving. There's no ham. And you two are so ungrateful!

I crease the wrapping paper into a wing between my nails. Father has not appeared and sister has walked out. I wonder what bird looks like this. Lizard? Mother slams the refrigerator. She wants me to look at her, but I keep my life between my nails.

I have never in my life seen someone look so ugly on Christmas, she says to me. What are those, slacks?! Do you wear them to humiliate me? So you can look like a bum in church! As if we didn't have any money to dress you! As if we couldn't care less about you! The one important day of the year, you look like that like, like shit. Do you like that language?

Fuck language! cries my sister, rushing back into the kitchen.

Joseph! Joseph! Joseph, come down here!

My mother screams. I pinch the two sides of my paper. Press gently and release. Make the bird fly. My sister charges the sink, falling over her short skirt and her pumps. She grabs a gingham dishcloth. Falls to her knees.

I'll serve you! she screams, I'll serve you, mother! Just look at me! I'll sit at your feet! I'll scrub the kitchen! I'll scrub the floors!

The floor. The counter. The floor. The counter. The floor. The counter. The floor. She is flapping. I fold. I pinch the bird. My mother grabs the cloth, breaks a nail. They are pulling the world apart at the seams on their heels. Poor Hercules dressed in a pinny. My sister, falling over her bondage, calls dogs with her squeals and I can't hear the pitch. Gang blast. Coyotes howl. I look away. Plates slip from the counter. My father is upstairs. He will not come down. He taught me origami. Grandmother's china.

the chandelier

This resembles a nightmare. Like a nightmare it is nonlocal: it is seeping, it has spread to the red hue of the furniture, to the channel on the television, to the Encyclopaedia Britannica's description of the big bang, to the smell of coconut oil in the polluted air, to the slim quality of light. There is a chandelier in the front hall. Touch it with your fingertips. I could reach it on tiptoe with my nails, if I jumped, with my knuckles. See the light explode, electricity on, smashed with my fist like words. Fractals of light fall from this chandelier. Look at the sun too long I will go blind, like they say about masturbation and God.

question

Where are you going? cries my mother.
I do not answer.

intention

I describe small people, contentious cripples. Maybe my disdain for these little clay figurines only partially formed and vulgar is classist, reverse prejudice and it is my Marxist tendency to put them in pots for sacrifice. But it is in fact my religious freedom. I am free to sacrifice on fire escapes.

question

I stand in the stairway.
Where are you going? she cries again.
I do not answer.

exorcism

To be free of ghosts, the Navajo say, fill a pot with water. But mama mama take me to the desert for I cannot be free of ghosts! Grind up a yucca root that has never been used for a hair wash. Grind up an ear of blue corn. Put these and your prayers in a pot with a lizard. First: her illiterate nose. Next: her fish-limp arms. Next: her neck. Next: her leg mapped with veins. Next: all stories. I will climb a high-rise. Fuck the nightingale, tear flesh with the eagle. Drop my pots from the twenty-first floor. Hail Mary while I'm waiting for the crash.

decision

I stand on the stairs, mother in the stairwell. Chandelier in the hallway. If I jump, all those rays of light like strips of paper fall.
  Where are you going?
  I swung hard.

newspaper clippings from the 1800s

Where are you going? a desert farmer asked his son who was crossing the yard long-faced with a length of rope. I'm going to make a swing. That afternoon, milking hour, the farmer found his son hanging in the barn, hands seized up around the neck, trying too late to make wishes. I read this story in my mother's antique sewing-chest, lined with the Gazette from the 1800s. I left this story intact and gently peeled off the remaining newspaper in careful strips: strip one: hangs a tale of empire, the preservation of favoured races in the struggle for life of handsome, old, grey-haired pioneers, makers of America, against the most diabolic painted Indians ever seen outside of the bottomless/two: pit, red wastes, fiery ore/three: did the Lord Judge among the Heathen, filling the place with dead bodies, harrows them, saws them, puts them to the sword and the most terriblest/four: sufficient light from the word of God for/five: city of good beer, mammoth oysters, and elegant niggers/six: brains of Washington raising a deafening shout of exultation in the opera house in/seven: times noblest off-spring/eight: Robinson Crusoe/nine: crusades again, whitening/ten: open the doors/eleven: our doors/twelve: our doors/thirteen: necessities of self - de/four-teen: destiny expands/fifteen: Jefferson's Unavoidable Destiny, Adams' Apparent Destiny, Polk's Manifest Destiny, Seward's Higher Law Destiny, Hays' A Cosmic Destiny/and many more strips that I could not read as they were stained brown-yellow with antiquity.

the chandelier

The chandelier shattered. Glass caught the corner of my eye, tearing three small holes into my eyelid. I heard my mother scream, Are you crazy? Stained glass, and the view of the cotton-wood holding buds against midwinter, forcing a fist in my purple mouth. While outside, wine did not pour for the winos. Go North. The unborn bore. Froze the foetus. I once had a tribe, said the Jew, bound together like notes to make a song. Silent nights slow lullaby, slurring words again. Bullets made the stars at noon on the news in Jerusalem. I could say the word forever. Jerusalem. Jerusalem. Our sweat making underground rivers. Lonely, come up through my veins, Saviour, and we will go deeper, soon forget about the birds in the sky.

Merry Christmas, I scrape my knees. Below me is the chandelier. Below me are the thousand shards of crystal, like a wave break over ice, descending circles of sound in a prehistoric canyon, a thousand tiny reflections taking emptiness as self, luminosity as other, a thousand words thrown clear across the carpet and snow across the fields catching the sun that my blood drips onto. My eyes are bleeding. Below me, there is light. And for a moment in this stairway, the winter becomes so silent you know that this is desert. Above me, one bare bulb continues to shine.

My father walks down the staircase. He is withdrawn from the reader, condemning the writer, he appears almost as a Puritan portrait holding a calligraphic sign, be silent unless your speech be better than silence.

He walks past us. My self, my mother, my sister, the dishcloth. He drips back into his armchair in the livingroom, his low lips and pink complexion, his burnt forehead against the lace head-rest, he sinks deeply. With limpid simplicity, desire for anything better passes out of him, unnamed. In a moment, it is gone.

I remember there being music in his voice when he finally spoke, for there was sadness in his voice, and he was not a man to show emotion except signed by the curvature of music. He said, Aren't you going to bed? I thought he would pass me his handkerchief to wipe the blood from my eyes, but he didn't. He turned slowly to the stereo and he put on his favourite 45. Stationed in Italy in the war, he had learned to love opera. Now, an Italian diva sang.

My father sank back into his armchair and remembered. The opera house was full. It was his first opera and it was always his first opera and the young man was a soldier. He climbed three staircases with extraordinary banisters. He sat awkwardly, crossed legs on velvet in the gods of the auditorium, pinching his ticket stub. So remote. In the far-off distance, he saw her white face flooded. He gasped. The diva, he said. With sound and light and fury and beauty and every eye adoring, she was singing, and the world should come to an end, now.

The newborn who died newborn will not become a ghost. He will become a blue bird, being spared by peace.

america

I was four, I was five. Turn the pages backwards. I tightened two metal strings on a miniature guitar and twisted the dangly bits on a birchwood wand. I invented music. I danced around the bed rattling and twanging in a short dress at seven a.m, unsure of my name. I didn't need a name. It was a promised land and I danced till I slept and I rose and I danced. Now memory listens to the pink room go silent night but the child is not falling into sleep. The night does not loosen the heat and the child sleeps with the window open. It is hot, it is cold. Soft wind and helium from the street vendor, a balloon moves slowly through the child's room. Sheer floral curtains drift over the window, there being no real nudity to keep from the neighbours, the child and the balloon are a shadow play.

The room is pale. There is a red ink print on the child's sheet. There is a riffling of voices out the child's window. There is a night bird whose love song is liquid. In the city fountain, he beats his black wings hard to walk, christ-like, on water. He calls like he will never again, his cry starting high, glissades down, pours sound into wells and pitchers of strong night. Hear the plummet? Hear the splash? Hear the song?

The child looks up from sleep just as the moon kisses the walls and saturates the boundaries of the pigment. Dark pink. Stuffed animals line the air-conditioner, a sheep-skin rug on the dress-up trunk, metal hinges and smell of mothball, a hand-woven rug, the child's first, more like an oven mat, hangs on the dark pink wall, and on the floor a doll's house with electricity and oak furniture, lights on in every room, dolls sitting in straight-back chairs, while a closet door swings open, a long mirror drips, smiling faces and vinyl feet adhered to the reflection, my reflection, beginning over, as if perhaps I could. I cover my child eyes with tiny ink-stained hands, bite my lip, wet my sheet, slip into the absent bottom of the world.

the whiteshell journal
changing

sex

Some Navajo say in the beginning there was One Word. Some Navajo say the word is gender, but the word is inaudible. Gender is silent until it becomes sex like lightning, splitting skulls when it touches ground. Some Navajo say, sex is dew. When the dews mix they tremble.

sex

I noticed the changes first in my room. Look up into the mirror and watch me grow, her girl-limbs pulling down from her tight sockets, down from her puckered joints aching into feet like little words. She says these words, and her face stretches. I see her eyelids grow. Her walk to the window brightened by fluorescence, and her ass rounds, nubile and sexy, it will turn my head. I see her from behind. City light lounges shadows down her back. The air-conditioner flicks on, on a timer. Thirteen. Fourteen. Let me take her through puberty abruptly. Thirty seconds. She leans back across her desk. She moves aside her child things, strips of coloured paper, a princess drawn in crayon, a crowded sketch of a circus, a dancing cow with one leg, a rider, a giant, his penis, a stocking on his head. She is fifteen. Time abbreviates. Her breasts swell from dimes, become worth paying for, catcall, someone howls from the street. She is not ugly. Her hair drags down to the small of her back and pulls on the lid of her scalp. She moans like she might throw herself out of the window. I see her framed in the open window, framed in the mirror. She takes on curves. She sweats ermine. She smells of cloves. She twists her hair in a knot to free her neck, sticks a pencil through the chignon to hold the bun. She imagines herself exotic and in and out of her body as if she could fuck herself when she becomes too lonely. I want to say, I'm here. She thinks it might be nice to fuck myself. She draws on the coarse brown hair beneath her armpits. She places her palm beneath one breast, lifts it. Tastes it. She discovers she can lay her own salmon nipple in her own orange mouth. The balloon moves several colours down the spectrum, across the deep shag carpet toward the pinkless wall and out the open window. She says her own name. She says her own name in many voices, rejecting each attempt to say her own name. She spreads her legs and sees in the mirror that her vulva has a face. Leans over herself, backwards. Breasts slip into a new formation, moons, at half cusp, circling a strangely inhabited planet.

earth

Down into the canyon, I can drop a stone and hear the stone descend in perfect silence. Down there, I know there is a river, but from here, only a snake, or perhaps there is nothing, as in the beginning there was nothing. In this land I can imagine perfect silence, the sound of sheep teeth on brittle grass. But every day I am walking with the sheep, goats and dogs and jet fighters practising mass destruction in the playground. Three useless dogs sleep and twitch beneath the juniper bush, their dreams running after jackrabbits, their dog-ankles snapping as they whine. One of my ewes has brain damage, was hit in the eye by a drunkard with a crowbar. Her right eyeball is purple silk, and it bulges from its socket, like a spider's sack ready for hatching. I imagine one day I will find the eyeball missing, its only trace a black cloud. A spider lays a thousand eggs on earth, all of them rise so gently. I want to go up with spiders and eagles. I want to change the colour of my eyes, like mutable sky and water, changing colour having none, and having none, inventing peace.

air (nilch'í)

In between the jet booms is a new kind of silence, a more audible silence because it is framed. I want to break it with a human song, a coyote's howl, a confession between the two, and the caseless wind. Always the wind is in the desert and always in the desert the sky is a dream. Wind, as the definition that I knew at the earliest age of my dreaming, wind meaning nothing, so this story must end with absence, wind meaning a destructive force, this story must end with ice, wind meaning air in movement, this story must end with flight, wind a breath, must never end completely.

I move the flock away from the precipice. On inaccessible cliffs a small herd of deer negotiate the incline and a potato-chip package folds in the wind. The sound is like the beating of wings heavy with wet blue clouds. Two goats join horns. I move them with my stick. The ewe with the bulging eye stands by the edge of the cliff. I cluck. She turns obediently and falls.

sun (johoonaa'éí)

The ewe cries out and its cry disappears into distance. Red flash breaking veins in my eyeball. As I reach for her, falling, I cannot feel the hand beneath me, lowering me, but something is lowering me. I am moving slowly or not at all. Only the land is moving, shifting browns. My back hunched like noon, my hand on the dirt, the dirt falling, but I am pinned to the ground. My back snaps, arches. The cold coming up from the ground hardening my nipples. My cheek on a pebble with a pointed shadow. With bent eyes, I see goat hooves. My neck twisted westward. Distance looks like water, this dried-up sea of desert. I see the sunset is round. Grasping at a stump, I try to stand, but I am pinned. Only the sun on my back in checkers, shadows of stones and weeds, the evening light as if the ground were burning. I try to stand, three times I try to stand. After the fourth time I try to stand, the sun descends upon me. The sun is a beautiful man. He lays his body across my striped back of wounds. And kisses it, in the final light.

water (to)

Is that your wet finger playing with my pubic hairs, parting my lips, my bloody hand slipping on the moisture, river? We live above the skies of four defunct worlds, I tell the river.

Spread your legs further, says the river. He is curious. Looking at my labia, my vulva, he has no names for my anatomy.

Each world has a colour's name, I say, staring up at the closed sky. Black World, Red World, Yellow World...

Which world is this? he interrupts, and pulls off two juniper twigs from an overhanging tree. Gently, like chopsticks opening a dumpling. My vagina.

Maybe I'm gonna have a baby but the child, only made of water, will die.

her voice over stalagmites

My desert mother says, Child of the Water, who was the twin of
Monster Slayer, cut his way out of the belly of a fish, he cut his
way out of the left side, and his head came through, out of the
right, his feet kicked. Child of the Water was the child of
Changing Woman. He came out and he stuck in it.

sex

My desert mother says it was like this: Changing Woman lonely
up an down. She out by herself every day. Big desert. An she
look up, there sun, an she look down to canyon, there river, an
she lie out on a big flat rock over canyon, legs open, watchin sun
go from his dawn house to his dusk house. She lay there as he
shine down hard on her brown skin an into her brown skin. He
shine down in and like in a dream, she lie with sun, happy, an
when he rise from her womb like dawn, she follow him up with
her big eyes blued and the sun gone travellin. He gone travellin,
an so soon it night again. She alone with achin in her flesh, and
the achin bring her down the canyon, an the achin send her
into the river. She lie down in the falls, in blue pool bottom,
with silver fish, green frog, water runnin through the splinter of
her legs, legs just openin round water, an the moon watchin and
reflectin Changing Woman. Lyin there, jus lyin, she touch the
water. She think maybe the water livin. Maybe water lonely too.
An water was. An sun was. An whenever sun lonely too, achin
for the Changing Woman, he leave a long footprint on the
dawn. An she come. An whenever water lonely it burst up in
one big wave an she come. Sun an water an everything beautiful
just love the Changing Woman, an pour up into her, an she
come, and she make twin babies who are the heroes come outa
her just like that.

birth

Birth was slow and stuck on the branches of winter trees, like
plastic bags one hundred million years later. Five worlds on.
From that tree, there hung a yucca rope and near the end of the
rope a large knot on which the woman gripped strongly the knot
of consciousness. Changing Woman's hair, loose from its ribbon
loop, sweated her shoulders and weighted the leaded night.

Behind her, a young man squatted, his arms circling her ribs, slipping on the sweat of her breasts. His face buried in her back, his eyes half open, he was looking at the river run down her long back. In his mind of water, he floated flowers down her long back. And his face bows into the cup of her shoulder. As he weakens, another man rises like the sun, and the two men exchange places behind the Changing Woman, turning beyond her, in a galaxy no one saw moving.

sex

I want to come. I don't want to say this to anyone. But I want to come, too. This is my silent list. I want the male bluebird gazing on me (this way I can see if I am beautiful). I want Tongue Mountain where the wind strikes speaking (this way, I can hear my voice through the tv). I want eyes rising time and again with sun over the mountain (this way in their eyes I can see me). I want speech begun as pollen (this way, I can talk about changing days). I want a home of moss, whiteshell, dawns, dark cloud like Changing Woman's home in the sky (when I go home to the suburbs, I feel homeless, and here I do not know where I am). I want a home in the west with Changing Woman (it hurts my body that things are outside my body). I want to go about with the beauty which covers the mountains and extends up their slopes (it hurts my body that I am alone, walking in the flat desert). I want to have a child born in summer, I want to roll him in the snow in the winter and watch snow melt.

birth

There were little children's footprints, belonging to the heroes, outside of Changing Woman's door. A monster came along one day and wanted to eat her children. Roar. Changing Woman asked, What children? The children of the footprints. Grrr. Oh those, she said, I made those marks myself, with my hand, because I was lonely.

a blue body in
the blue-horizon-light

time

air unveiled of heat dawn cannot get out night turns inward and closes space no view sky folds wings see she says this is the last world a locust hatched in the night in the dawn a fresh shout in the starched grass its blunt head cicada under the drum time changed she walked threw a bucket of water into the sky water splashing back herds drunk at the pool where the river stops

dropping into motion longing in the drips of the fall twirl my finger in the swirls we are moving quickly through time and story between eight walls I want to be a bird and not me this day telescoping days into one day soon there is such a confusion of tense time expands contracts here or there wherever it lies these days will be done like a never-ending-snake

they go on they went on there were many hoops to pass through white hoops of aspen one white of wild rose mountains seen to be white even in the spring

the dead

Everything is disappearing very quickly. On the sand, ants scared away by wolves and in the suburbs, mommy talks about ants all the time: jelly ants, leaf-cutter ants, harvest ants on their hind legs. She is afraid of being born an ant in her next life. Mommy does not actually believe in reincarnation, but she fears it. She begins itching at the thought. She squirms in bed and father sleeps on the couch. She says she does not want to become an ant. She will do anything not to become an ant. She tugs at her eyelids as she says this. Her eyelids are becoming distended. In her next life, statistically, mommy is more likely to become an ant than any other creature. Of known species, fifty-five percent are insects, fourteen percent are flowering plants, nine percent algae, fungi, and ferns, eight percent non-insect anthropoids, eight percent invertebrates, three percent vertebrates (us), and two percent bacteria and protozoa. Thirty species of roundworms live in each human stomach. What percentage of life is parasitic? How many other creatures die when a human exits?

my father and the dead

Everything is disappearing quickly and not much time has passed. Five o'clock, my father dissected a pocket watch that had ceased working since Woodrow Wilson. Coils all over the kitchen table. It is on the whorls of fingertips that the ghosts remain. Five o'clock, my mother began serious drinking. By seven o'clock my father cooked pizza, regular fare on burnt nights. Two hours of passing liquor into her small body, my mother was bombed. My father had learned about pizza while stationed in Italy during the war. That night, the moon was particularly strong but no one took account of it under the street-lamps. At seven-thirty, listening to Verdi, pizza in the oven, springs and coils and tiny wires, impossible to put the watch back together, my father had a stroke. Officially, he went to hospital and lived one night and one day. Unofficially, he never left the kitchen full of music, the needle lifted, having never really been present without music. The room paled to the violin. The second-hand lodged under his thumbnail.

the dying

In the morning, the family gathered at the hospital. My sister, by this time, had a fast car and a loose husband. She had married at eighteen and she had always been older than me. They had a baby and I didn't. They arrived at the hospital in the fast car. I imagine they made loud driving noises to go quicker and amuse their baby. Now their baby sat on the hospital bed and I thought maybe I could trade its life for my father's but didn't know who to approach. Meanwhile, my sister and her husband filled the sheets with gifts. They brought the dying man a stuffed koala and chocolate amoretto cherries, having forgotten that father hated chocolate amoretto cherries, but pleased to have shouldered the expense. With wrapping and ribbons and a lot of politeness and mother actually in clothing, everything appeared like Christmas, and father was the Christmas tree, red tubing up his nose and through his veins. To his right, a machine flashing green lights telling us This Is A Special Occasion, Appear to Be Happy for Soon it Will Be Over. The evening sun cut through the gap in the drawn curtains, a single shaft slipped into the hospital room, so the syringe on the shelf gleamed silver, tin bowls polished, glasses winked, artefacts changing with the hour glowed kindly, became dishonest and corrupted, while my sister's baby reached for the light and discovered nothing but his own hands, radiant.

dying with music

I brought my father a Walkman. Father had heard of such things but had never inspected one. Technological innocence is not so unusual for a professor who scoffed at aluminium poisoning, demonized the Cuisinart and eulogized old vinyls. He was an old man, old fashioned, and regardless of what his students wore or did, he was outrageously nearsighted. In his world, not much had changed: wagons were not a great decline from cars, time was just behind us and in front of us it remained, amorphously, time. His body dying, only a further stasis: recorded history.

I placed the headphones on my father's ears, brushed away the few grey hairs and turned the volume up slowly, trying to avoid the unavoidable shock. His mind exploded. His eyes scrolled up toward the cork ceiling of the sickly room, looking for cracks, looking for the entrance of angels. Where is the music? he asked repeatedly, no rhythm in his breath. Where is the music coming from?

I pointed to the small cassette and he didn't believe me. For the first time in his life, there was no intermediary, no gap, no air. Like his easy idea of heaven, there was music all around him. Gradually, he relaxed in this non-being, began to conduct, 2/4 time, 3/8 time. His fingers, no good with matter, caught every entrance of voicing in his ear. Reaching the crescendo, he pulled out his IV.

The nurse replaced the IV and the headphones. An angel sang soprano in my father's ear and slept with him that night.

dying with angel

He was no longer speaking or moving. At sunset, the family left for gin and tonics. I stayed behind, leaning through the hospital window, watched the station-wagon which they entered like little ants. There's a bird's nest in the saint's hand on the Catholic Foundation wall, I said to father. He could hear nothing. Saint Sebastian was a martyr. One black tree. Echo of the moon in the crescent on a mosque. The garbage and the street lamp. The beggar. A boy. A saint. A mosque. A bus stop. A road. A wall. Graffiti, written in red and crossed out in blue. What word is that? I asked my father, but he was far away.

I leaned out further. Who signed his name with a slash through it? I felt the night wind on my neck. Who is thinking words and knowing they are always about longing and crossing them out and knowing the crossing out is still more about longing? The quiet room was wheezing through the cork. I sat in a plastic chair in the corner. More contagious than open space, the corner smelled of disinfectant, giving hope. As long as the soprano sings my father will live.

There was a small plastic pouch into which his urine drained. I imagined his urine as yellow tears like a smoker's tears. I would have caught his tears in my coffee cup, to protect him from witchcraft, but there were no tears. I have never seen my father cry. He was fathered by a suckling absence, someone wrote. I knew my father would never curse me and never love me, and instead he would disappear into death entirely, like an origami bird unfolded.

Somewhere, outside in the sky, in the stomach of one nighthawk, were five-hundred mosquitoes. Somewhere the flowers closed and opened their petals, caught between night and preparation for morning, when the desert does not bloom and the moths lose their riot of night colour, become drab, folded over and unnoticed. Unnoticed, an angel entered on the yellow light of the street lamps, sound of a car engine and what we wrongly call silence as the words that should describe this scene passed like smells of cooking out the window. It was so simple. With black wings, the angel leaned over my father's chest and dripped blood from its mouth onto his nightgown. What are you doing? I asked the angel. Dying, the angel said.

my father's psalm

...and he will raise you up on eagles' wings, bear you in the breath and he will raise you up on eagles' wings, you need not fear the terror of the night...

sandpainting

In the hogan the medicine man pours yellow sand between his finger and thumb forming a rainbow border for protection of the painting and the patient. The rainbow remains open in the east. Where the pure sun rises, space is impermeable towards evil.

Draw snake, he tells me, placing a pinch of blue sand between my white fingers. Triangle is cornpatch, he says, three lines is corn root. His bowlegs tremble. He says, marry me, and maybe for a moment he means it. Eighty-two years since his milk teeth fell out.

A wristwatch plays Land of Dixie at ten o'clock, and Land of Dixie at eleven o'clock, and at noon a kid scrapes a knife blade up his bicep, bored. His father is sick. Swollen in the gut, for any of a number of reasons: he spat or ate in a tornado's path, or a small twister whirled through the yard and caught him around the belt. Now he lies on the earth, shivering in a blanket.

Zigzag lightning, says the medicine man, do yellow. I mimic his old-paint-fingers pouring sand in a plumb line, sun beam, drop pendulum of a grandfather clock through arthritis. He makes no mistakes; he must make no mistakes, omit nothing from the complex design, forget no colour-order; he must recreate the past and present simultaneously. Perfect language, perfect image, perfect repetition cannot fail.

The medicine man pours down sand like someone placed the mountains, just so, and so, he places them again, like it is easy. Understand, daddy?

the dead

Tonight my father's buried. We avoid consciousness in the livingroom. Maybe death needs noise, maybe death needs television, but no one is ever honest enough to turn it on. My brother-in-law tucks the baby under his armpit and swings. Hear the whoop. Await the crash. Imagine flying or at least levitating. Hear the baby on the ground again, shuffling. Hear the sound of the baby's finger and thumb between which he takes a sardine from the carpet, dropped there from dinner. Smell it. Hear him raise it, strong contemplation, no language, the habit of mystics.

The family has been to mass. Blessing of the earth. Blessing of the casket. The word-made-flesh breaks down in our mouths at communion as the moon is shattered by technology. I took communion, like a cat stealing sardine heads from a half-opened tin in the trash. The cat will never be wounded by edges. Christ was not the first-born saviour, Death was. Moon rise. First night my father's rotting. Who will sharpen a can-opener on this pussy's tongue?

mouth and blood,
red pigment

prayer sticks, as obligatory invitations to the gods

I want to force the gods to enter my world. Sometimes the gods enter the beginning as if the beginning were a location, sometimes they only enter the end. It is too late for the beginning. I had a grandfather, a grandmother, but I am left with speculation, word prisons, terracotta dust, lace shreds, illness. No one to tell me. A dead song like a bird behind glass in the museum of the one dimensional. Books, flat as dust. Nobody.

Once, I believed that my family had a history and this history had produced me and, in turn, I had accumulated a past like barnacles on a maiden voyage and these barnacles, occasionally, under the romance of sunset, resembled jewels. I tied on my grandmother's black bonnet, which was bad luck. In time and heat it dissolved into black ash that I smeared beneath my eyes to darken them. Rub charcoal on my face, drive ghosts away. Iron ore, startle them off with glitter. Red ochre if I'm pale, make me appear whole and untouchable, holy.

Now the jewels change shape and colour continually and I am not certain whether they are in fact there or not there or whether anything that I thought was one thing was not another thing all together. I have changed the colour of my eyes completely. In the desert where little appears at first sight, time happens without warning. Autumn plumb-drops. In the desert where there are no leaves to fall, God is a metronome only. The sound bl-bl-bl-bl made after every song set.

black (ljin, lyinígí)

Black grants invisibility. Thus, protective and sinister. Its corresponding precious stone is jet. Sometimes black is the northern colour of evil and danger. Sometimes eastern. Sun has the power of Black Wind. Black Wind hid Sun's anger. In a terrible storm, Black Cloud, staked by rainbows and sheet-lightning, and Black Fog, staked by sunbeams and zigzag lightning, protected Changing Woman. Sun gave Black Wind to his son, Monster Slayer. Black God is all black in the dance. Monster Slayer's body is blackened for battle with black coal of Dark Sky. Blackening is a rite to frighten ghosts or foreigners or enemies. Black denotes origin. Black Corn is all the corn in the universe and the origin of corn. The Black Endless Snake is all snakes in the universe and the origin of snakes. Black Thunder, all thunder and origin of thunder. The Place of Emergence, which is the hole between the worlds is black.

red (ltci, litci'ígí)

Red is blood, and flesh, and the colour of danger, war, and sorcery. When Monster Slayer clubbed to death Travelling Rock, his mouth and blood became red pigment. Child of the Water is painted in red ochre.

pink (disos)

A quality of light. Featured in the Bead Chant, which is Scavenger's chant. Colour of eagles. Colour of the human trying to reach the sky or the water.

figure painting ('akina'adzoh) further identification

from the Shooting Chant

During akina'adzoh, the patient is naked. She covers her mouth with her hand — Navajo gesture of shyness. There are men present, but it is me she looks away from as the medicine man paints her body. He paints blue sun between her brown breasts, paints white moon in the middle of her back. From the sun and the moon he draws lines down her torso, around her waist, over her shoulders, across her spine. Lines like a harness, holding her breasts which are loose and low, though the nipples are hard. It is cold outside because of me, and because of me she bites her lip. I have brought all this. Washing my hands this morning, I splashed water outside the door and brought rain today. I woke late, and clearing the house, dumped ashes from the fire after sunrise. Dumping ashes on the sun, I brought bad weather. My mother says do not bring cornmeal macaroni into the hogan or I will bring hail, too.

The medicine man paints lines on the woman's chest like a binding to hold snatches of hay or a baby, and so free her arms for work. On her arms, he draws four black clouds edged in white, like snow I think and heroin I think. It is a deranged thought. These are the distant metaphors of a fixation. Black colour is made from the soot of roots. His swirling fingers. Her skin pressed and filling. Her pallet. Her pores. He paints a snake on her foot. It bites her big toe. Fang, scraping the dirt. Snake's house on her instep. He smears red salve on her hard jaw, black on her eyes. Here you touch her body, he says to me, and her hand goes to her mouth.

actual paintings

My desert mother sleeps in her prairie-skirt. I curl close at night and steal her heat. Does she wear underpants? When she herds, she herds on foot, not horseback, because wind bad, she says, wind gonna blow her skirt up over her head. But she doesn't have a horse anymore. She says if she had a horse she'd slaughter it for me and feed me good. She cooks fry bread, cornmeal mush and mutton. Eat, she says, hungry? (The horse was slaughtered years ago.) We come up from starvin, we go back to starvin, she tells me. Once, people almost rich with sheep, an the US govment think our sheep eat too much so the US govment send the Sheep-Reduction Posse. Don't say they comin to kill our sheep. Don't knock on our doors, say, scuse me, you wanna pick out the worse sheep an give a butcherin an eat all you can with all you family, cause don't mean to bother you, Miss, but you got too many sheep an some gotta die. Don't say that. They not sayin nothin all. Just come. Grandma walk one morning to the water-hole with her kids an her sheep. Everyone chasin dawn to the water-hole this mornin. An US govment come on horseback. Cavry everywhere. Cavry herdin the sheep into the washes, ditches, anywhere they can. Cavry throwin gasoline on our sheep an burnin our sheep alive. A shepherd get real mad, throw a stone at a US horse, and the US rider hit the shepherd with a rifle. The shepherd fall to the dirt like a snake, twistin and streakin with blood.

how do I understand this world?

It is not arithmetical. It is a world of coiled rope. It is not a world of the four food groups, of species, races, kinds of rock. It is a world of run-on sentences returning to my mouth. This world is beaded on my wrist. My mouth is wet, my wrist is hot and wetness and heat, the Navajo say, give birth, a never-ending snake. It is a world of subtle linkage greased with rain-water and verbs. In what sentence does one word have to do with another? They do what gives me sense, the opposing logic. By logic you cannot touch me but all my senses are alive to yours. Breathe here, my neck will purr. Logic is stationary and cannot make a world that spins but fingers can. Weave, warp, paint, carve. This world twirls whatever way. This world draws into its axis. As in the downpour, a spider makes a cluster of drops.

categories

Here is a cluster of drops, a small example of how Navajo thought is organized: what makes a group, what makes a whole.

example: east.

The direction east has the jewel jet. The east is fastened by lightning, is clothed by daylight. No one can tell me why it was that the black bird sang over morning, but the black bird did sing, so the black bird is of the east. Red, white, and blue corn, not making a flag but a rainbow at dawn, is also of the east. The sound of the east is thunder four times. The people of the east are numerous. They are rock-crystal boy, girl, whiteshell girl, boy, dawn boy and girl. I understand dawn boy and girl. But dawn and whiteshell are the same. Rock-crystal is the same. These boys and girls move together and apart over sentences and stories merging, separating, carried by spotted winds. Spotted wind is the wind of the east. An untranslatable god is the tutelary of the east.

There is thunder in young eagle's mouth, today. Whiteshell with a belt of dark cloud. They called that monsoon.

sex

Jack's just some boy I met in school in the suburbs. We're walking through ploughed fields of watermelon. Something pastoral
is growing in the seams of the field, sheep in the corner of my
sun-blind eye, sheep like teeth around the circled enclosure or
battleground of barbed-wire and overripe bleeding watermelons.
I say, Eat the wind, and I open my mouth. Taste it? I ask, and I
offer Jack my mouth.

Jack and I step over barbed-wire. He pulls it down, squeezes
his fingers between barbs, yellow and dungy fleece on the snag of
fencing. We say nothing much. I could run my finger down
these barbs like a grand piano, curve my shoulders, cock my
head, show off my collarbone, but I want this empty, awkward...
a false sentence and repeated silence that is the beginning of
what will happen next.

A coyote howls strange at midday, unnerving, and I sing very
quietly. I am not very good at singing and it is a very small song.
I sing about lilacs in New England and then the song goes dead.

The air force, Jack says, call them California condors.

What? I ask. I look for distractions, incidentals, tumbleweed,
twirls in my hair. What are you talking about?

The jets, he says. See them coming over the hill there?
Condors eat carrion you know.

I know, I say.

Condors are like vultures, he says, they're bald.

I will speak quickly, before the jets erase it all. I say, There's a
holiday in Peru called Condorachi. It means the Tearing of the
condor. The bird is hung alive by its wings under a public arch-
way. The men mount horses. They take pass after pass at the
condor, hitting at it like a pinnate. They beat the condor with
their fists till the condor's dead. And the man who strikes the
last blow bites out the condor's tongue. Its tongue is long and
yellow and it carries the same bacteria as rotten meat. That's all
the ugly man thinks of. He doesn't think how the condor is a

beautiful bird that was once a human who wanted so much to learn how to fly she turned herself into a bird. I stop, breathe, say, I always think jets are crows before the noise, they fly so low.

Five hundred feet, Jack says. A ewe runs deafly sideways. Marching, he adds and laughs. The wind catches a grain of black-ant-sand, raises the grain and lands it on Jack's right eyelash, so precisely as I have seen his eyes.

Look at you, I say.

What about me?

Nothing. The human became a condor and learned to fly, I say again. Then the condor taught all humans how to fly. Sun peels the skin on my neck. The condor is almost extinct in this country, I say. I ply a flake of skin off with my nail. Who will teach me? I ask. How I look in Jack's eyes, and how I stretch. And I stretch and stretch as if by extending my body to the desperate poles, red sun and red earth, the red wind between, I would fly.

I let down the Navajo loop of my long red hair. Smiling, I shove the white ribbon in my pocket. It slips from my pocket and now, at a distance, I mistake it for bone and leave it on the earth. Tuck my hair behind my ears. One strand, riding through the loop of my earring, falls on my breast.

Jack steps forward. I laugh tightly. He touches my hot neck, takes hold of a strand of my hair. I laugh smally. Slowly, he pulls me toward him slowly, inch by inch, laughing, a little tighter, a little harder between my toes, here, ants, in the background, sheep, goat, large bird, laugh, buzzard, or an eagle or a hawk, circling laughter, condor, somewhere my mother, and beyond that crows becoming jets, wind, laughter, he pulls me closer, then he stops. And we laugh. I feel desperate.

And I cover my ears. I am bending. We are swaying. We are pulling into each other when the jets sweep down. I rip off my shirt and he lifts my breasts. This is a soundless scene. Driven by the blast, my head disappears into his hard crotch. The jets come one after another, howling low, one after another and another. Behind the noise, looking up from his groin, I read his open lips. I see up over his belly, his round chin, his cropped black hair: jets, four, five, count them. A crow dropping. A drill, six. A black flock, seven, eight. Velocity crumbling the early moon above an uninhabitable tract, while my red head burrows, Jack's fingers on my zipper, my hands over my soft broken ears.

I spread my thin legs widely as the speed of the bird is checked in the opening and spreading of its tail. In all the changes which birds make in their directions they spread out their tail. The spreading and lowering of the tail and the opening of the wings at the same time to their full extent arrests the swift movement of birds. (Leonardo da Vinci) He moves his penis inside me. He rolls me on top of him. Maybe I will fly.

mother

All this was a part of a never-ending-snake, as the Navajo believe that all secrets, especially those of sorcery, are divulged, involuntarily, during sexual intercourse.

How you do that!? she shouts. How you be so stupid!? (She stands beyond the fire. Shadows dance the walls. Out the smoke hole, stars are closing. The moon crumbles. Dinner falls off the plate and ants ascend from the floor. She has knocked over the coffee pot with an angry hand. As it pours into the earth, dirt rises around it like a carnivorous flower.) How you think that stupid boy have anything to teach you!? How you think that little boy have anything to teach you!? How you give yourself away!? How you give earth away!? How you give away Changing Woman!? How you give him things not even yours!? How you give him parts of gods!? How you give him parts of me!? How you tell him things not even yours!?

I didn't tell him anything.

They not even yours! You Anglo! He Anglo! He ugly an he gonna do somethin ugly with what he know now! How you ever gonna get holy now!? How you ever gonna get knowledge now!? You crazy! You jus crazy now! You in him now an you aint comin out! You a part him now! Me, I a part him now! You understand me? You don't wash him off. He in you. You in him. Sex do that. That what sex do. It make you same. An he not good, he not holy. He just some boy, some stupid ugly anglo boy an now he part you! He pour hisself into you! You him now! You understand me! ? How you not love no one!? How you give your body away like shit!? Like shit! Like it yours to give away!

What? Whose body is this then, yours, God's, whose? (I'm crying.)

Fool, you not even made a woman yet!

What? I am now. What do you think I am now?

Monsters be born inside you. Only monsters born without love.

Stop it. Don't say that.

You want me tell you story? You always want me tell you stories? You wanna know more Navajo way so you can tell all you
people! Okay. I tell you story. Once, there was a very bad chief
an he got a very bad daughter. But she weren't so bad as he was,
she was jus stupid. An the bad chief was real mad at his daughter
who made a monster cause she so stupid. So he cut off her nose!

    You're lying. You're making it up.

Then he cut out the vagina an penis of the Wind, cause the
Wind bad, too. The Wind wanna suckle the baby monster at the
Wind tit. Cause Wind love monsters. Cause Wind love jus anythin. Wind gonna pick up anythin. Gonna drop it when he
bored. That the Wind. The Wind don't care. But now Wind was
mad. Wind was real mad to have its vagina an penis cut off like
nothin an blown away like a couple of Christmas tree after New
Year. So one night. You listenin me, I talkin you, you listenin?
One night, Wind dance round the fire of the Chief. There ain't
no stars in this sky that night, no moon in this sky, an no way out,
only coyote howlin and owl huhuhuhu, but there's a big Wind
dancin, wavin its tongue. I gonna be Syphilis now, say Wind to
the Chief, I gonna be Spanish Pock, I gonna live under the
North, I gonna be the People of the Cold, an Rottenness, I gonna
carry Plague on the storm now, nothin gonna move me, no
prayers, there gonna be no songs to me to move me, I got no ears,
I don't hear you, nothin. You hear me, nothin. It like that. You
hear me? It get ruin easy. It delicate. It the world. It get ruin easy.

the colour black
when it is placed in the east

We are weaving. Coloured wool and it is raining. The monsoon is purple. The lightning is green. These like jets come and go. Rain gliding over the caked sand, running into cracks, opening fissures like thought. In the hogan, my desert mother and I listen to the drumming of the rain. Outside, if there were worms they would be bleeding. Rain like fists. I wonder what war is like. Weaving as the sky pours and thought is endless. My desert mother, weaving the pattern of the world for the tourists, leaves herself a spirit hole in the rug, to escape. Hoohoohoohoo, the waters moved. She's strung a second bed frame so we weave side by side and she says, hear god?

Hoohoohoohoo.

What's that? I ask.

In the beginning, there was no creator, she tells me, but this god called out the beginning and this god was a word giving birth but the word is unheard of. Get it? Hoohoohoo. God or owl. Some say, in the beginnin there was One Word. Some say in the beginnin there was colour. Word or colour, same colours we weave with an speak with.

She twitches the expanding and deflating corners of my awkward rug. Loom. Night come. Moon. Pull tighter, no not that tight, she says. Colour move in emptiness, empty black, empty white, empty blue an empty yellow. When black an white met in east, First Man created with white corn an dawn at his feet. When blue an yellow met in west, First Woman created with yellow corn an sunset. They didn't get along. They talk like breakin pots. Still raining outside. Lightning. We weave red as well, an unweave red, as well. But the world didn't feel so empty anymore.

As we weave and it rains, I tell her how my ancestors crossed the Atlantic. I tell her about the famine, about grandfather leaving and grandmother following, never finding him. Eating slugs.

Working in the abattoir in Brooklyn. The illegitimate baby.
Child of the devil. Or an angel.

Child of Holy Man? she asks.

No, not Holy Man. About going west. I tell her everything I
know or have forgotten creating. The Irish smoked dudeens, I say.

What?

Pipes. They brought them from Ireland. Women smoked them.
Like us, she says.

Not for ceremony, just for habit, I answer. I don't know, they
didn't bring much from that world.

What they bring? she asks.

Rain beat. Rhythm of the string between sentences. A rug
beginning to take over patterns. Shawls, I say, shoes, I say,
dreams, prejudices, lullabies, fiddles, I don't know, I say and tie
an end off, cut it with my teeth. Fear of ghosts, foreigners, devils, witches, I don't know, everything. She turns the oil lamp
higher. Superstitions, I say, fairies, goblins, poverty, strange
recipes for sheep. Sometimes they brought husbands, sometimes
wives, sometimes children, and sometimes all these were left
behind and the Irish just threw everything up and became
Americans. I don't know. It was a long time ago. But there is no past
tense, and is my language faulty? It is raining and will it ever stop? From this
mud room, imagine all the graves in the world are unearthed by monsoon.
Monsoon and jet fire. Ireland, floated with corpses. Flouted with history.
Whose? The digs. Go down go down. All worlds have their juices. But how far
before I hit rock? I want to know. I want to take what is mine from yours, from
the dead and gone. Sometimes I would like to be a witch. Maybe sometimes it is
necessary to be a witch. Out here, only witches touch the dead with impunity.
Only witches can grave-rob and survive it. Witches dig up a corpse, shrink it,
blow on it, stretch it, screw it, take its power, take its story from its skin. I don't
want to do that. I don't want to talk. So taboo, the Navajo never speak of the
departed. I want to, but when I think I want to, it is as if I killed them myself.
Who? How? Begin in a bog full of bodies. Write open that ledger of First Earth
and call it A Tribal History. Look down. Everyone was dying in 1863. But my
grandfather was not a gravedigger. Did I have a grandfather? He was a peat-cut-
ter. I am the digger. I am the robber. Listen to the rain and the rain's echo. I am

I am Scavenger Scavenger who who picks these words from any tongue like precious garbage from any book of answers. My grandfather sunk to his waist at the end of the world. My grandfather lifted a shovel and disappeared. My grandmother spat on the Bible that my grandfather had left behind him, along with seven children and debts and she took up witchcraft, she made it her legacy. She closed the door on his non-entrance. She cursed him forty days and nights running. It keeps raining. It keeps raining. But maybe she didn't curse him, I say. I'm making up words because I don't know what my grandmother said. Though I think she would have cursed him, having left her to die. I have no one to tell me. Rain beat. Where is the bard with his stick, pounding out the beat like the malt from the barley, singing my story into existence? I have my grandmother's bonnet, I say. Sometimes I tie it on my head at night. It's black.

You funny girl, she tells me. Black unlucky.

speech, the colour-wheel and world-emigration

First Man and First Woman carried their bundles of both good and evil from one world to the next pushing up through the crust to this final world. This world-of-many-colours delirious with desire and fever and words. It was progress. The previous worlds were small and unsuitable to humans because humans kill when the world is too small. The previous worlds were known by their colour: Black World, Red World, Blue World, Yellow World. In this last world, light replaced colour.

I say worlds but they weren't really worlds. I forge a loose translation to make appropriation simple and avoid fear. The word sa'ad is used to refer to each world. But literally, sa'ad means speech. Beneath our many voices are dead voices, each of a single colour, words destroyed by flood and fire and famine and war. Black Speech, Red Speech, Blue Speech, Yellow Speech, like lightning fingers on the burnt horizon tonight.

sickness

in white

By October my mother went to live in the Clinic for Alcoholics. By November she had moved to the Hospital for the Mentally Disturbed. The professionals had dried her up and found there was nothing there but her worst fear, like a black apricot. When I see her now, I try to remember her as she was. She looks nothing like her photographs in the stairwell, the one on the seventh step in her wedding dress, the eighth step in her snug black number, killer stilettos, velvet gloves. She has changed, of course. My mother's grey bottom emerges from between the ties of her white hospital gown. She wears frayed toeless slippers. I bring her new slippers for dignity. I have to place them on her feet to show her how.

She does not speak. She stares at the thick black ants eating wax off the red peonies. Their mouths full, they descend the stem, the frosted vase, the stainless steel table. They climb the walls and disappear in corners. Mother has pulled out many of her eyelashes. She scratches her palms till her skin bleeds and ugly stigmata break through. Her wounds smell of rubbing alcohol and sweat.

I would like to touch her body when she writhes, I would like to clasp her hand, but the slightest touch drives her deeper into the space in her guts and the emptiness in her brain. So I sit on the orange plastic seat by the metallic bed like the chaise of a Ford, fold my hands in my lap like I did as a child waiting for chocolate pudding. Like a spoon my mother curls her soul, frightened, into her flesh. Of all eating utensils, the spoon, in particular, resembles the body folded in upon itself, cast down.

She is looking at white walls, white internment, and perfunctory red flower. She longs to leave the world of man's events: time. She longs for god's non-event: space. She longs for madness to complete itself in pure consuming retreat: an inverted oasis, a mirage, in which what appears empty is full, what appears decaying and mortified, returned to it origins, to nothing, is in fact unbounded, breathing, but hidden so deep within itself, so acclimatised to the deathly, that it will happily take shelter in a carcass.

Madness is better than suicide. It is a sudden and sustainable death, one without hell, one without heaven, one without the possibility of rebirth into any of the one of the hundreds of thousands of God-forsaken creatures.

This is a shared room. The other patient eats and sleeps behind a blue synthetic curtain on aluminum runners. She is younger than my mother and has tried to kill herself. Sometimes an older woman comes to visit and brings her a Big Mac. The smell of the Big Mac infects everything, including the flowers. How come they all fuck me and no one wants to love me? the patient asks weakly.

Cause yer a cute little hippie girl, bloated on heroin. (I think this is her mother talking.) In that shit hole apartment of yours, you can't even drink the water. Who's gonna make a life with you? Baby, you're a junkie. Don't snarl. You don't gotta like me. I wanna be a lady but I'm never gonna be passive again like I was with your father. When I started talkin, I started cursin. (I don't know how much my mother hears of her neighbours' conversation. She stares at the fluorescent light, accustomed to its delicate buzzing.)

black

There are thousands of lights in the city distance but one light only in the desert. I walk at night.

Between juniper cracks and mud, if I squint, I can see a bright fire, and my mother bent away from my gaze, the hoop of her back stretched over a loom. I am outside. Smoke is snatched from the tin chimney into the northerly, gale force ten tonight, stub limbed trees bent like souls all around me and dog tails tucked, whimpering. A small body runs by on four crook legs in the black, barks.

Inside the hogan, my mother looks up and closes the curtain across her door so her candle will cease to drip, steady without a draft. She returns to her weaving. She is weaving the cliff of the dead, but the trader and his buyers will never know that. Black triangles, red background, hung in a fashionable livingroom.

This is what I learned: to bury a person who is not quite dead yet, pray like this: talk about the victim's head, chronicle the different body parts, move downward. End the prayer in the ground.

Through the mud slat, I see her pause. She sits up straight. Then she stands up. She unbinds her hair which is looped by a white ribbon. She opens her fingers and the ribbon flies away. Her black hair pours down her spine like a long road. She blows out the candle. Black.

With the particular beauty of silence, I run my hands along the splintered gate. You can hold death like rain in your palm, it is so delicate, spilling through your tight fingers.

the wall

Wind pushes me, cries my name, curses my name as if my name were significant. Wind takes my shoulders and, with giant hands, forces my name into my body and I cannot hold its weight, I crumple, a sudden indentation in the wall of night, I seem to fall endlessly into time. See, this is my head spiralling down, all lights in the city are human now and my eyes like two dead planets. Curtains close in the desert. Wind's up. A star has shot and disappeared.

fever

I bite my little finger. It bleeds with delirium. Red ants race down the sheet. I am sick. This is the law of slingshot-animism: if you do it wrong, it will come back to you. I have done it wrong whatever it may be. Fever 106 degrees. The shits. Vomits. Hallucinations. In my eyes all shapes stink of snakes. Evil in the arrow snake, flying snake, bull snake, stubby rattler, and grandmother rattlesnake shakeshakeshake. Mothermothermothermother.

My mother says, hush now hush now, you got fever, girl, quiet.

There is evil in the bite of the red ant mouth. There is evil in the red ant vomit. Evil in the razor white cactus, in the bumblebee and mud-dauber sting in my brain. They say that I have ghost sickness. They say I have been witched, say I am a witch, and the witching has returned to me. Bang.

My mother says, no no, you jus done it wrong.

But what have I done wrong?

Everythin.

Without initiation, I should not partake in a ceremony, I should not touch the holy sand, I should not help the medicine man, I should not pretend to sing/mutter when I don't know the words, I should not ask so many questions, I should not act like I understand the answers. I am too weak to withstand the power. I should not learn so fast. The white anthropologist died of a paralytic stroke while studying the Night Chant. I should not be so good at weaving the first-time weaving, I should not be weaving so much, too much I am out of order, I should not be precocious, or I am out of balance, I should not be so brave, so unafraid of the dark, only witches and ghosts are not afraid of the dark.

You are a witch? How do you know? What are you doing here? Why did you kill your parents? Did I? Why did they let me? I am just stupid. I am just confused. You must know what you're doing before you do it, if you don't it will be believed you do. People thinking I have knowledge, I am not as I appear. My culture teaches me to look like more than I am. I am not I am not I am not I am not a buzzard is is is the head of the witches is is is the beanshooter.

Are you a witch?

Who says so?

They think you a witch.

Never dream about the dead. Do not brush your hair at night. Never sleep on a buffalo skin or you're engaged to the man who lent it you, or are you looking for a husband? They say you have no mother which means you have no morals. You should not have bad dreams or what is real? You should dream about a horse. You should dream about a well. You do not know the outcome of knowledge out of order.

She says, eat this, you be better.

What is it?

God.

pezograph: stimulent drug used ceremonially to induce visions.

pezograph: pits suggestive of fingertip imprints that are common on meteorites coming down.

You shush now, girl, shush now... My mother lays the dawn upon my body. She picks the vomit from my hair. A heavy wet rag on my forehead. Smell of brown coffee in the hogan. My desert mothers watching me sweat through the glassy air. I need to shit. Her body behind mine, her arms under my armpits, holding my ass over a bucket. She catches my shit in a bucket. Shh shh shh shh shh, she says, pouring yellow cornmeal through my white fingers.

dream

Wind swallows you. Wind cries you. A door slams shut, hinges creak, slams shut again. It is wind, it is not your mother. There is no one entering or exiting the desert except the past and present and future gathered here tonight in the repetitive tense like a heart beat, and all your ghosts of years of history are gathered here tonight. Don't be afraid of ghosts now that you are one. See warriors again and weavers again and bead-makers again and hand-tremblers again and bone-suckers again and medicine-men again and horsemen again and shepherds again and hunters again and soldiers now convicts now cowboys now hobos now government officials now blacksmith now forger now potato-farmer turned corn-farmer now bog-farmer turned desert-farmer now gunsmith now ironmonger now whore now seamstress now barman now doctor now tax-collector now all unnamed wives now undertaker now vampire now ant-man now bird-man now woman and your grandmother in her black bonnet. Wind clears the land of useless characters. Let the land be free, let the land be fertile or infertile, it doesn't matter as long as it is ours, your ancestors say, stepping off the boat and into the coach and west and west and west again and again in the desert you walk alone hearing voices slipping like a sail from the tight harness of these words, luffing, white, ripping, crack its sheetwhip on northern clouds for from this hard sky there will be no exit and will be no entrance, will be no heaven's answer, no gentle rain, because

here God let you go. Go, He says to your ancestors, Damn yourselves. And you do.

And He is weeping for everyone I know. And his tears are
mad and his tears are sharp and his tears will come like an army
of four thousand as my ancestors came and came and came and
did not wash up on the shore and die in little foam like a wave-
break on Manhattan and his tears will continue inland from the
eastern coast, cutting streams under hedges, rivets of ploughed
fields, carry off seedlings down forest footpaths, carry off
saplings, acorns, dried pine needles and spotted bird eggs, clear-
cut the hawthorn crest of the Puritan Cemetery, through the
wrought-iron gates of the Catholic Foundation, smoothen gran-
ite, smother history, and flow down the ditches of new and old
graves for all of them are His who has thrown them down into
ditches and He will throw them up again, carry their bodies off
in floods of history, follow their course from wheel track to highway, from pasture to flatland to desert where once bodies
entered and made so many corpses that mountains trembled and
waters fled and ghosts were born that could not love and for
what is left living and naming itself America, and naming itself
worthy, and wealthy and one nation under who... there are
many worlds beneath us and this one floods.

Tomorrow will hear the echo of the wind and the bats will become confused.

in blue

It was very white and smelled like white things. There were two beds, well tucked. There was a rolling formica table for both inmates. Sometimes there were red flowers on the rolling table. Outside were cacti which bloomed only at night, rock which didn't bloom and sand for many miles. Wind, yellow, passing over.

I actually enjoyed visiting mother. Sometimes when I went to the hospital, I saw brief glimmers of awareness in her. I said to the nurses, in the spoon lies the wind, which must have sounded crazy. I know they thought I was crazy, my mother's daughter, and so, I began to fear my visits to the hospital. I began to suspect the doctors and the nurses were waiting for me. They were chronicling potential remedies: whistling over patient, patient holding bow and arrows sitting on the big white star, pollen administration, hoops of red willow being used as black snakes for transgression, ashes blowing (audience participation), brushing the patient's head with the word be'be'. And always being sure the patient is aware that the whistle represents the reed through which the hero breathed on his journey to the Sky.

I began to wonder whether a bed had been reserved for me, its hospital corners snug, a training-nurse bouncing a penny on its white sheets. Whether someone in a pale blue dress was now taking a black magic-marker to an index card, pausing, wondering how to spell my name and finally giving up and drawing a picture instead. Whether all this care was being prepared for me right now at my insurance's expense. But I was adamant and I kept talking. I believed there remained near my mother some small wind, a wind with a blinking eye. And the wind's eye watched over her madness. And it whispered, I am still here, oh look at you, how you long to leave me.

Behind the runner and the curtain, as I have said before, there was another hospital bed. The heroin addict had been released and I heard that when she got home she actually managed to kill herself. Now, for one day, there was a young and beautiful man in her place. At least I think he was a man. I was surprised the hospital mixed sexes in communal rooms, but I believe there was temporary overcrowding. The full moon. In fact when I returned the following day, the man was gone. I never saw him again.

He was crazy. He ate his beauty whole with his simple mouth carving curses that I imagined might kiss me tomorrow like Jesus returning the favour to Magdalene. The air filled with his curses. I would have liked to have kissed him to move this tale toward anointment, but there were many hands of demons in his mind wearing sheer plastic gloves, fixing metal vices to his gums, stretching rubber over his lips, and he was pulling off his face, screaming, don't shush me!

A nurse turned away, walked down the white hall in the white desert calling to the other white nurses, bring drugs. The man scowled. He pulled down his face like a mask. For a moment, he was incredibly, unbearably ugly. His brainwaves moved beyond my comprehension, and my words aestheticize neurochemistry, call it ugly, for I am only a noviciate of beauty. I know nothing.

After the drugs, as after an orgasm, his face returned, became gentle. He started weeping. His arms reached up to heaven, flapping, fingers playing the air softly.

Hush now, hush now. Let me hold you to my breast, I said, drawing back the blue curtain that divided us. My mother continued to stare at the ants. There was piped music all around us. I am ruined! he wept and I imagined I had ruined him. I said, Forgive me, I have only seen a man cry once and that man made vomiting noises and spilled whiskey down his cheeks, but I have seen boys cry often, and angels, and saints, and the insane; which one are you?

But the plastic syringe, full of clear liquid, had put him to sleep already, and I watched him disappear behind water, behind glass, slowly dripping, being the thickest liquid. Can I wait that long, draw in my hand through a single drop when the seam comes loose? Or can I simply enter now?

My desert mother says, when you sleep on the sheep skin, you gotta sleep with your head on the tail. Don't you ever sleep with your head to the head, or that sheep gonna carry you away in the night.

dream

My words are like dreams, being awake they should be ugly like the neurologist instructs me, too many delta waves, like children sleeping, but to me they are beautiful, not being mine. My words are like dreams, unrecognized by the world that passes not knowing what is hidden is open, is flying, is crossing continents, calling for heaven lit up with closed eyes, plunging inward, upward, and where does breath go exhaled? My words are like dreams in which I dream that I do not dream but lift a paper into flight and the waves rid themselves of the sea, become a desert. I have someone else's dreams in me, a scavenger's dreams in me, not knowing myself, not knowing him, but dreaming myself dreaming him. Stepping out of words that will lead to the future, to the airport, where I take one step further into the icy water, we are on the same continent, twenty miles from the border of heaven, his storm strikes me one day later, the continuum of time, common history, runs through our feet, he takes one step closer, my words are in the air, his dreams in me begotten. Flying in his dream for me, raining in his dream for me, just beginning in my dream, remeeting in our dream, crashing on bedposts and impostors in the dream, testing for breathing, we both have dreams in our dream, it doesn't matter anymore, he says in my dream, it has changed cliffs, lips, in dreams, masks, changed mouths in my dream, looking south, going down in the earth in my dream to the maggots, how firm is the fall, how deep is the drowning, the scream rising, the words in flight, in our dream, broken.

My desert mother finds me sleeping in the sand. First, she unclenches my fists, then she wakes me.

What am I now? I ask.
You are fifteen, she says.
And I don't know how to fly yet.

echo

...the sound of the echo is reflected to the ear after it is has struck, just as the images of objects striking the mirrors are reflected into the eyes. Just as a stone flung into the water becomes the centre and cause of many circles, and as sound diffuses itself in circles in the air; so any object, placed in the luminous atmosphere, diffuses itself in circles, and fills the surrounding air with infinite images of itself.

(Leonardo da Vinci)

the hollow

The end of the story is they all kiss and make up. So I have no tongue, as some say of ghosts.

So the sound of the kiss appears to come from the cottonwood, high from the juniper, high from the pinon pine, aspen, joshua, sagebrush, squawbush, saltbush, yucca plant, night-blooming cerus blooming red with blood, ocotillo, paloverde and the corn plant that is growing yellow up my forehead and the bluebird that lands there, now.

And the sound of the kiss is also low, so low it seems to come from my shadow, where the sidewinder lives and the scorpion lives and the gila monster lives and the diamond-back rattlesnake lives and the coral snake lives and bites and kills and resurrects and sings as the sun rises suddenly and extends darkness behind all objects.

And the sound is distant and seems to come from my memories gathering in a hogan folding legs to ears and minds to sky, as the smoke rises quickly through the smoke hole that is the exit from the world or the entrance.

And the sound is also present and seems to come from one that only opens her mouth and, because she has no tongue, only ice angels form on the air.

dream

I draw down my shawl and unzip my coat. Doing this, the sky twists white. It is snowing. I am wild. I am frowning at the end of the world. And all is buried. At the desert lake, I tap on the ice, where fish are cased in silence. No bird sings over my nails, over my head, where heat escapes into the loam of the white sky. Nothing above to see me. Look up from my reflection.

I sweep the snow from the ice with a broom of cattails. Seeking my likeness in the distortion of strata. There, and there, and there again, as mercury descends. I pull out my knife and cut a hole in the ice, as if to catch a sleeping perch that will break in the leap toward the sun and slap its tail on the sky. I have never heard a fish scream.

In America, there is such a noise, such an interminable cry of our own desire, we cannot hear our screaming. I do not know what is a vision and what is a dream and what is death and what is simply longing. In the desert, I can hear my own silence. A single human lowering sound like a magnet into and out of her throat, hearing herself through the ear-canal entering her body. Light, in and out of my eyes.

I have cut a hole the size of my torso in the ice. I have undressed. My chest contracts as if I desired the cold, and perhaps I do. My nipples red. I am naked and I will enter the water. Doing this, my flesh twists white and I will not mar the perfection of snow. A red eyelash forms an icicle. My eyeballs burn and swell. And the whorls of my toes, and the arch of my instep, my ankles, my calves, my kneecaps, the soft behind my knees, my thighs, my hips, my fat, my pelvis, my hair, the folds of my pale vagina, my next-born child, my clitoris, my joy, my womb, my door, my shit, my piss, my belly, the knot of my small umbilical cord, my waist, my gut, my fear, my stomach, my liver, my bile, my high thin breasts, my strong nipples, my lungs, my shoulders, my tetanus scar like a frozen kiss, my collarbone I covet in mirrors, my simple neck, the dent in the base of my neck where fingers will touch tomorrow when I meet tomorrow o o my chin be' be' my lips my kiss my tongue here here is my tongue my teeth my spit my phlegm my snot my nose the bridge of my nose my eyelash my eyeballs my iris my visions and all I have seen my ears my tunnel my entrance my exit my memory of the sound of my breath in my head go in and out my air through my head my mind my thought my question my sky

Other titles from Insomniac Press:

Room Behavior by Rob Kovitz
(cultural studies/architecture/non-fiction)

A woman sits alone in a darkened boiler-room. A man enjoys hanging suspended from the ceiling. A dirty room indicates the secret sexual proclivities of its occupant. A curtain rustling in the breeze portends fear and paranoia.

"The purpose of a room derives from the special nature of a room. A room is inside. This is what people in rooms have to agree on, as differentiated from lawns, meadows, fields, orchards."

Room Behavior is a book about rooms. Composed of texts and images from the most varied sources, including crime novels, decorating manuals, anthropological studies, performance art, crime scene photos, literature, and the Bible, Kovitz shapes the material through a process of highly subjective editing and juxtaposition to create an original, fascinating and darkly funny rumination about the behavior of rooms and the people that they keep.

5 1/2" x 7 1/2" • 288 pages • trade paperback (162 B&W photos) • isbn 1-895837-44-8
Canada $19.99/U.S. $15.99/U.K. £11.99

The War In Heaven by Kent Nussey

The War In Heaven collects the latest work from Kent Nussey. A unique blend of the stark realism of Raymond Carver and the Iyrical precision of Russell Banks, Nussey's writing levels the mythologies of an urban paradise with fictions that are humorous but dark, touching and dangerous. In this book nothing is sacred, secure, or safe. Comprised of seven stories and a novella, *The War in Heaven* explores the human capacity for desire and destruction in a world where everything condenses beyond metaphor into organic connection. For Nussey love is the catalyst, creating the currents which sweep over his complex and provocative characters, and carry the reader to the brink of personal and historical apocalypse.

5 1/4" x 8 1/4" • 192 pages • trade paperback withflaps • isbn 1-895837-42-1
Canada $18.99/U.S. $13.99/U.K. £10.99

Dying for Veronica by Matthew Remski

A love story of bizarre proportions, Matthew Remski's first novel is set in Toronto. *Dying for Veronica* is a gritty and mysterious book, narrated by a man haunted by a twisted and unhappy childhood and obsessed with the sister he loves. This shadowy past explodes into an even more psychologically disturbing present — an irresistible quest and a longing that can not be denied. Remski's prose is beautiful, provocative, poetic: rich with the dark secrets and intricacies of Catholic mythology as it collides with, and is subsumed by, North American culture.

5 1/4" x 8 1/4" • 224 pages • trade paperback withflaps • isbn 1-895837-40-5
Canada $18.99/U.S. $14.99/U.K. £10.99

Carnival: a Scream In High Park reader edited by Peter McPhee

One evening each July an open-air literary festival is held in Toronto's High Park. It is a midway of diverse voices joined in celebration of poetry and story telling. Audiences exceeding 1,200 people gather under the oak trees to hear both well known and emerging writers from across the country, such as, Lynn Crosbie, Claire Harris, Steven Heighton, Nicole Brossard, Nino Ricci, Al Purdy, Susan Musgrave, Leon Rooke, Christopher Dewdney, Barbara Gowdy, bill bissett... This book collects the work (much of it new and previously unpublished) from the 48 writers who have performed at Scream in High Park in its first three years.

5 1/4" x 8 1/4" • 216 pages • trade paperback withflaps • isbn 1-895837-38-3
Canada $18.99/U.S. $14.99/U.K. £10.99

Beneath the Beauty by Phlip Arima

Beneath the Beauty is Phlip Arima's first collection of poetry. His work is gritty and rhythmic, passionate and uncompromising. His writing reveals themes like love, life on the street and addiction. Arima has a terrifying clarity of vision in his portrayal of contemporary life. Despite the cruelties inflicted and endured by his characters, he is able to find a compassionate element even in the bleakest of circumstances. Arima has a similar aesthetic to Charles Bukowski, but there is a sense of hope and dark romanticism throughout his work. Phlip Arima is a powerful poet and storyteller, and his writing is not for the faint of heart.

5 1/4" x 8 1/4" • 80 pages • trade paperback • isbn 1-895837-36-7
Canada $11.99/U.S. $9.99/U.K. £7.99

What Passes for Love by Stan Rogal

What Passes for Love is a collection of short stories which show the dynamics of male-female relationships. These ten short stories by Stan Rogal resonate with many aspects of the mating rituals of men and women: paranoia, obsession, voyeurism, and assimilation. Stan Rogal's first collection of stories, *What Passes for Love*, is an intriguing search through many relationships, and the emotional turmoil within them. Stan's writing reflects the honesty and unsentimentality, previously seen in his two books of poetry and published stories. Throughout *What Passes for Love* are paintings by Kirsten Johnson.

5 1/4" x 8 1/4" • 144 pages • trade paperback • isbn 1-895837-34-0
Canada $14.99/U.S. $12.99/U.K. £8.99

Bootlegging Apples on the Road to Redemption
by Mary Elizabeth Grace

This is Grace's first collection of poetry. It is an exploration of the collective self, about all of us trying to find peace; this is a collection of poetry about searching for the truth of one's story and how it is never heard or told, only experienced. It is the second story: our attempts with words to express the sounds and images of the soul. Her writing is soulful, intricate and lyrical. The book comes with a companion CD of music/poetry compositions which are included in the book.

5 1/4" x 8 1/4" • 80 pages • trade paperback with cd • isbn 1-895837-30-8
Canada $21.99/U.S. $19.99/U.K. £13.99

The Last Word: an insomniac anthology of canadian poetry
edited by michael holmes

The Last Word is a snapshot of the next generation of Canadian poets, the poets who will be taught in schools — voices reflecting the '90s and a new type of writing sensibility. The anthology brings together 51 poets from across Canada, reaching into different regional, ethnic, sexual and social groups. This varied and volatile collection pushes the notion of an anthology to its limits, like a startling Polaroid. Proceeds from the sale of *The Last Word* will go to Frontier College, in support of literacy programs across Canada.

5 1/4" x 8 1/4" • 168 pages • trade paperback • isbn 1-895837-32-4
Canada $16.99/U.S. $12.99/U.K. £9.99

Desire High Heels Red Wine
Timothy Archer, Sky Gilbert, Sonja Mills and Margaret Webb

Sweet, seductive, dark and illegal; this is *Desire, High Heels, Red Wine*, a collection by four gay and lesbian writers. The writing ranges from the abrasive comedy of Sonja Mills to the lyrical and insightful poetry of Margaret Webb, from the campy dialogue of Sky Gilbert to the finely crafted short stories of Timothy Archer. Their writings depict dark, abrasive places populated by bitch divas, leather clad bodies, and an intuitive sense of sexuality and gender. The writers' works are brought together in an elaborate and striking design by three young designers.

5 1/4" x 8 1/4" • 96 pages • trade paperback • isbn 1-895837-26-X
Canada $12.99/U.S. $9.99/U.K. £7.99

Beds & Shotguns
Diana Fitzgerald Bryden, Paul Howell McCafferty, Tricia Postle & Death Waits

Beds & Shotguns is a metaphor for the extremes of love. It is also a collection by four emerging poets who write about the gamut of experiences between these opposites from romantic to obsessive, fantastic to possessive. These poems and stories capture love in its broadest meanings and are set against a dynamic, lyrical landscape.

5 1/4" x 8 1/4" • 96 pages • trade paperback • isbn 1-895837-28-6
Canada $13.99/U.S. $10.99/U.K. £7.99

Playing in the Asphalt Garden
Phlip Arima, Jill Battson, Tatiana Freire-Lizama and Stan Rogal

This book features new Canadian urban writers, who express the urban experience — not the city of buildings and streets, but as a concentration of human experience, where a rapid and voluminous exchange of ideas, messages, power and beliefs takes place.

5 3/4" x 9" • 128 pages • trade paperback • isbn 1-895837-20-0
Canada $14.99/U.S. $10.99/U.K. £9.99

Mad Angels and Amphetamines
Nik Beat, Mary Elizabeth Grace, Noah Leznoff and Matthew

A collection by four emerging Canadian writers and three graphic designers. In this book, design is an integral part of the prose and poetry. Each writer collaborated with a designer so that the graphic design is an interpretation of the writer's works. Nik Beat's lyrical and unpretentious poetry Noah Leznoff's darkly humorous prose and narrative poetic cycles; Mary Elizabeth Grace's Celtic dialogues and mysti cal images; and Matthew Remski's medieval symbols and surrealistic style of story; this is the mixture of styles that weave together in *Mad Angels and Amphetamines*.

6" x 9" • 96 pages • trade paperback • isbn 1-895837-14-6
Canada $12.95/U.S. $9.95/U.K. £8.99

Insomniac Press • 378 Delaware Ave.
Toronto, Ontario, Canada • M6H 2T8
phone: (416) 536-4308 • fax: (416) 588-4198
email: insomna@pathcom.com
web: www.insomniacpress.com